THE CASE OF THE

Fabulous Fake

BOOKS BY

ERLE STANLEY GARDNER

The D.A. Takes a Chance   *The D.A. Breaks an Egg*

THE CASE OF

The Fan-dancer's Horse	*The Long-legged Models*
The Vagabond Virgin	*The Foot-loose Doll*
The Lonely Heiress	*The Calendar Girl*
The Lazy Lover	*The Deadly Toy*
The Dubious Bridegroom	*The Mythical Monkeys*
The Backward Mule	*The Singing Skirt*
The Cautious Coquette	*The Waylaid Wolf*
The Negligent Nymph	*The Duplicate Daughter*
The One-eyed Witness	*The Shapely Shadow*
The Fiery Fingers	*The Spurious Spinster*
The Musical Cow	*The Bigamous Spouse*
The Angry Mourner	*The Reluctant Model*
The Moth-eaten Mink	*The Blonde Bonanza*
The Grinning Gorilla	*The Ice-cold Hands*
The Hesitant Hostess	*The Mischievous Doll*
The Green-eyed Sister	*The Stepdaughter's Secret*
The Fugitive Nurse	*The Amorous Aunt*
The Runaway Corpse	*The Daring Divorcee*
The Glamorous Ghost	*The Phantom Fortune*
The Sunbather's Diary	*The Horrified Heirs*
The Nervous Accomplice	*The Troubled Trustee*
The Gilded Lily	*The Beautiful Beggar*
The Demure Defendant	*The Worried Waitress*
The Lucky Loser	*The Careless Cupid*
The Screaming Woman	*The Queenly Contestant*
The Daring Decoy	*The Fabulous Fake*

Erle Stanley Gardner

The Case of the
Fabulous Fake

HEINEMANN : LONDON

William Heinemann Ltd
15 Queen Street, Mayfair, London W1X 8BE

LONDON MELBOURNE TORONTO
JOHANNESBURG AUCKLAND

First published in Great Britain 1974
Copyright © 1969 by Erle Stanley Gardner

434 28226 x

Printed Offset Litho and bound in Great Britain by
Cox & Wyman Ltd,
London, Fakenham and Reading

Foreword

FOR many years, my Perry Mason books have been dedicated to leaders in the field of courtroom medicine. For the most part, these people have been forensic (courtroom) pathologists (experts in disease and injury), whose skill in determining the *cause* of death helps convict the guilty and protect the innocent.

Cause of death is always a medical question.

Manner of death, on the other hand, is never a medical question. If, for example, the *cause* of death is a bullet through the head, the *manner* of death is whether it was self-inflicted, accidental or fired by another person in the commission of a crime.

Jack Cadman, Director of the Orange County Sheriff's Criminalistics Laboratory in Santa Ana, California, is an expert investigator in determining the manner of death.

One of his early cases dealt with a young woman who had been fatally shot in the back with a shotgun. There were two prime suspects, the husband and one of his friends. Cadman asked for the clothing that each was wearing the night of the shooting. He found microscopic droplets of flesh and blood embedded in the sweater of the boy friend, the man entered a plea of guilty, and the case was solved without even the necessity of a trial.

A short time later, a proverbial "hired" man was found dead in a barn. His crushed head looked much as if he had been kicked by a horse. Jack Cadman examined the man's hair and scalp, and discovered tiny fragments of dust and a few wood splinters. This initiated a search through a huge wood pile for a two-by-four which, Jack suggested, ". . . may be three feet long." It was found, and examination under the microscope disclosed fresh depressions caused by the head hairs being pressed into the compressed wood. Hairs and micro droplets of blood from the victim's head confirmed that this was the weapon that had caused the death.

A suspect was found; robbery was the motive; and another guilty plea to murder resulted.

Jack Cadman is internationally known for developing the Cadman-Johns method for detecting alcohol in the blood stream through the use of the gas chromatograph. This method is perhaps the most accurate one developed to date. A test can be completed in fifteen minutes, whereas other methods require from one to four hours.

Cadman is in great demand as a lecturer at scientific meetings and at universities throughout the West.

He has just moved into a modern and well-equipped

crime laboratory which is a real show place, illustrating what science can do in evidence that will tie a criminal to the scene of his crime.

"The solution of the crime problem has to be the field of science," Cadman said, as he surveyed his stereoscopic and ultropak microscopes, his refractometer, search and sweep tables with their vacuum attachments, and a dozen other new crime-fighting tools. "This is the space age, but crime-fighting has not kept pace with other scientific developments since World War II. Any time the American people are ready to give the problem sufficient attention and priority, we can raise the present 'solved' and 'conviction' rates from maybe 10 percent to 90 percent. When it becomes unprofitable for a criminal to commit a crime, he's going to think twice or three times about doing it. When he knows that the odds are nine to one that he's going to get caught and going to jail, crime will lose a lot of its appeal. But until that happens, why shouldn't people continue to commit crimes? It's quite a profitable trade!"

Therefore, I dedicate this book to an outstanding leader in the field of forensic science:

JACK CADMAN
Director, Orange County Sheriff's
Criminalistics Laboratory
Santa Ana, California

ERLE STANLEY GARDNER

Chapter One

PERRY MASON looked up from his desk as Della Street, his confidential secretary, stood in the door of the office which communicated with the reception room.

"Yes, Della?"

"We have a young woman in the outer office who won't give her name."

"Then I won't see her," Mason declared.

"I understand how you feel about these things," Della replied, "but I think there's some interesting reason why this young woman won't give us the information."

"What sort of reason?" Mason asked.

Della Street smiled. "I think it might be interesting to find out."

"Blonde or brunette?"

"Blonde. She's holding on to a flat black bag in addition to a purse."

"How old?" Mason asked.

"Not over twenty-two or twenty-three."

Mason frowned. "Are you sure she's over twenty-one?"

Della shook her head. "You can't tell by looking at her teeth," she said, smiling.

"How about her hands?" Mason asked.

"And you can't tell too much by a woman's hands until after she passes thirty," Della explained.

"All right," Mason said, "bring her in, we'll take a look."

Della Street turned, went into the outer office and shortly returned with a young woman who was trembling with excitement as she approached the desk and said, "Mr. Mason?"

Mason smiled. "There is no need to be nervous," he said. "After all, I'm an attorney and if you are in trouble perhaps I can help you."

She seated herself across the desk from the lawyer and said, "Mr. Mason . . . I . . . I . . . I'm going to have to disappear and I don't want my parents ever to be able to find me."

Mason regarded her thoughtfully. "Why are you going to have to disappear?" he asked. "The usual reason?"

"What's the usual reason?" she asked.

Mason smiled and shook his head. "Don't cross-examine me," he said. "Let me do the questioning. Why do you want to disappear?"

"I have my reasons," she said. "I don't think I need to go into all the details at the present time, but I do want to disappear."

"And you want me to help you?"

"I want you to be in such a position that you can, if

necessary, furnish the missing link which will connect me with my past life. But I don't want you to do it unless I give you permission and tell you to, or unless certain circumstances develop which will make it imperative that you do communicate with my parents."

The telephone on Della Street's secretarial desk rang and she said, "Hello . . . yes, Gertie. . . . Right away? . . . Is it that important? . . . Very well, I'll be right out."

She glanced meaningly at Perry Mason, said, "If you'll excuse me a moment," and hurried through the door to the outer office.

Mason regarded his visitor quizzically. "You're asking me to take you on trust."

"Don't you have to take all of your clients on trust?"

"Not entirely. I usually know with whom I am dealing and what the score is."

"And you are usually retained to defend some person who is accused of crime?"

"Quite frequently."

"And how do you verify the fact that your client is telling you the truth?"

Mason smiled. "You have a point there," he admitted.

"You take them on trust," she said.

"Not entirely," Mason replied. "Any person accused of crime, whether guilty or innocent, is entitled to a defense. He's entitled to his day in court. I try to give him legal representation."

"But you try to make that representation effective so that you prove his innocence."

Mason thought for a moment, then, choosing his words carefully, said, "I try to make my representation effective. I'll go that far."

Della Street appeared from the outer office, motioned to Perry Mason, and walked through the door into the law library.

Mason said, "You'll have to excuse me just a moment. We seem to have some rather important matter demanding immediate consideration."

"Certainly," she said.

Mason swung around in his swivel chair, got up, walked around the desk, gave his visitor a reassuring smile, said, "I'm satisfied it will only be a moment," then opened the door to the law library.

"What's the excitement?" he asked Della Street when he had closed the door.

"Gertie, at the switchboard," Della said.

"What about her?"

"I hardly know," she said. "You know Gertie, she's an incurable romantic. Give her a button and she'll sew a vest on it every time, and sometimes I think she even uses an imaginary button."

Mason nodded.

"She observed something about our visitor in there, or thinks she did, and perhaps you'd better talk with her."

"Can't you tell me what it is?"

"Of course I can," Della said, "but I can't evaluate what Gertie's saying the way you can—it makes quite a story."

"All right," Mason said, "let's go see what it is."

He took Della's arm, escorted her through the door which opened from the law library into the entrance room.

Gertie, at the switchboard, was sitting on the edge of her chair, her eyes wide with excitement, her jaws chewing gum in a frantic tempo, indicative of her inner nervousness.

Gertie had an insatiable curiosity. She always wanted to know the background of Mason's clients and, quite frequently, vested them with an imaginary environment which, at times, was surprisingly accurate.

Considerably overweight, Gertie was always going on a diet "next week" or "after the holidays" or "as soon as I return from my vacation."

Despite the fact there was no one in the office, Gertie beckoned Mr. Mason over to her desk and lowered her voice so that it was barely audible.

"That young woman who went in your office," she said.

"Yes, yes," Mason said, "what about it, Gertie? Did you notice something about her?"

"Did I notice something about her!" Gertie said, quite obviously savoring the fact that she had for the moment become the center of attention. "I'll say I did!"

"Well," Della said impatiently, "tell it to Mr. Mason, Gertie. After all, she's waiting in there."

Gertie said, "You noticed that black bag she's carrying with her, that she hangs on to so tightly?"

"I didn't notice her hanging on to it so tightly," Mason said, "but she has both a black bag and a hand purse with her."

"It's a kind of cosmetics and overnight bag," Della said. "In a bag of that type there's a mirror on the inside of the lid when you open it."

"And cosmetics, creams, and hairbrushes on the inside?" Mason asked.

"Not in *this* bag," Gertie asserted vehemently. "It's packed, jammed solid with hundred-dollar bills, all neatly packaged."

"What!" Mason exclaimed.

Gertie nodded solemnly, obviously enjoying Mason's surprise.

"How do you know, Gertie?" Della Street asked. "Tell him that."

"Well," Gertie said, "she wanted to get something out of the bag or put something in it. Anyway, she opened it, but it was the way she opened it that attracted my attention."

"In what way?" Mason asked.

"She turned around in her chair, her back toward me, so that I couldn't see what she was doing."

Mason smiled and said, "And the minute she did that you craned your neck, trying to see what it was she was concealing."

"Well," Gertie said, "I guess everyone has a natural curiosity, and after all, Mr. Mason, you want me to find out about the clients that come to see you."

"I was just making a comment," Mason said. "Don't let it worry you, Gertie. What did you see?"

"Well, what she didn't realize," Gertie said, "was that just as soon as she turned her back and opened the lid of the bag, the mirror at a certain angle reflected the contents of that bag so that I could look right into the mirror and see what was inside."

Mason said, "Tell me exactly what you saw."

"The whole inside of that black bag," Gertie said impressively, "was just one mass of hundred-dollar bills, all neatly stacked in piles just as they came from the bank."

"And you saw that in the mirror?"

"Yes."

"Where were you?"

"I was here at my desk by the telephone switchboard."

"And where was the young woman?"

"Sitting over there."

"All the way across the office," Mason commented.

"That's right. But I saw what I saw."

"You say she turned her back to you?"

"Yes, very ostentatiously."

"And then opened the bag?"

"Yes."

"And when the lid reached an angle of approximately forty-five degrees you could see the contents of the bag?"

"That's right."

"Now, did she very carefully hold the lid in that position so you could continue to look at the contents, or did she open it the rest of the way so the lid was straight up?"

Gertie thought for a moment and said, "When I stop to think of it, I guess she opened it the rest of the way, but I was so startled at what I saw that I didn't realize she had opened it the rest of the way until you asked me just now."

"Then she held the lid which contained the mirror for some appreciable interval at that angle of forty-five degrees so you were able to see the contents?"

"I guess she must have, Mr. Mason," Gertie conceded. "I didn't think this all out until— My heavens, you cross-examine a person so!"

"I don't want to cross-examine you," Mason said, "but I do want to find out what happened. You must admit that if she opened the lid of that bag and then held the mirror at an angle so that you could see the contents, she must have been rather anxious for you to see what was in the bag rather than trying to conceal it from you."

"I never thought of that," Gertie admitted.

"I'm thinking of it," Mason said thoughtfully.

After a second or two, he went on. "How did you know they were hundred-dollar bills, Gertie? You couldn't see the denomination at that distance."

"Well, they . . . they looked like hundred-dollar bills, all flat and—"

"But they could have been fifty-dollar bills?" Mason asked as Gertie hesitated. "Or perhaps twenty-dollar bills?"

"Well, I distinctly had the impression they were hundred-dollar bills, Mr. Mason."

"And, by the same sign," Mason said, "looking at those bills in a mirror across the length of the office, they could have been one-dollar bills?"

"Oh, I'm *certain* they weren't one-dollar bills."

"What makes you so certain?"

"Just the way they looked."

"Thanks a lot, Gertie," Mason said. "I'm glad you tipped us off on this. You did quite right."

Gertie's face lit up. "Oh, I thought I had botched it up, the way you were asking those questions."

"I'm just trying to get it straight," Mason said. "Forget all about it, Gertie."

"Forget about something like that!" Gertie exclaimed. "Mr. Mason, that woman is . . . well, she's going to lead you into *something*. She just isn't any ordinary client."

"That's quite right," Mason said. "She isn't an ordinary client, which is perhaps why the case intrigues me."

The lawyer patted Gertie on the shoulder. "You're a good girl, Gertie," he said. "You just keep an eye on these clients that come in, and if you see anything unusual always let me know."

Mason nodded to Della Street and they went through the door into the library.

"What do you think, Chief?" Della asked.

"I think Gertie saw the contents of that bag, all right, and I think it was packed full of currency. But whether it was filled with hundred-dollar bills or whether it was filled with one-dollar bills is anybody's guess. I don't think Gertie could have seen the hundred-dollar denomination at that distance while looking in the mirror."

"Gertie has a wonderful imagination," Della said.

Mason nodded thoughtfully. "But," he said, "the important thing is how long that mirror was held at a forty-five degree angle; whether our mysterious client *wanted* Gertie to see what was in the black bag and report it to us, or whether she was taking something out and Gertie's quick eye managed to get a glimpse of the contents. . . . You have to hand it to Gertie for that; she can see more in a tenth of a second than most people can see after staring for five minutes."

Della laughed. "And then her mind has a computer system all of its own by which she multiplies what she has seen by two."

"Squares it," Mason said, laughing. "Well, let's go back and see our client."

Mason and Della returned to the lawyer's private office.

"I'm sorry we kept you waiting," Mason said. "Now, let's see, where were we? You wanted to have a lawyer who would represent you in case you needed an attorney?"

"That's right."

"But you didn't want anyone to know your identity."

"I have my reasons, Mr. Mason."

"I presume you have," Mason agreed, "but that makes it rather unsatisfactory as far as I'm concerned. Suppose you want to communicate with me so I can do something for you. How am I to know that I'm talking with the same person who retained me?"

"We'll agree on a code," she said.

"All right," Mason said, "what do you suggest?"

"My measurements."

"Yes?" Mason asked.

"Thirty-six, twenty-four, thirty-six," she said.

A smile flitted across the lawyer's face, then he was serious once more. "That's not much of a code," he said.

"But if I gave you the measurements in my own voice over the telephone—you'd recognize my voice, wouldn't you?"

"I'm not certain," Mason said. "I might. Sometimes voices are rather hard to place over the telephone. What would you want me to do? That is, what do you think you'd like to have me do if I should decide to represent you and you should call me over the phone?"

"Defend me," she said.

"For what?"

"Heavens, I don't know," she said, "but the people who are trying to find me are very, very ingenious. They wouldn't go to the expense of hiring private detectives when they could accuse me of having committed some crime and put the police on my trail. *That's* what I'm afraid of.

"You see, Mr. Mason," she went on hurriedly, "I'm not at liberty to tell you all of the facts, but there are certain people—that is, a certain person who wants to find me or who might want to find me. That person is devilishly ingenious. He would stop at nothing."

"It's not easy to find a person who deliberately disappears," Mason said.

"I know," she said, "and this other party knows that,

too. He isn't going to waste his time and money hiring private detectives at fifty dollars a day. He'll accuse me of some crime and get the police to find me."

"And then?" Mason asked.

"Then," she said, "I'd have to defend myself."

"You mean he'd actually try to press these trumped-up charges?"

"He might. He might try *anything*."

"He would be putting himself in a very vulnerable position," Mason said. "That is, unless you *have* committed some crime."

"But I haven't."

"What do you think he would accuse you of?"

"Heavens, I don't know. Murder perhaps. He's absolutely ruthless."

Mason eyed her steadily. "Or perhaps embezzlement?" he asked.

A sudden flush of color flooded her face.

"Well?" Mason asked.

"He might even do that," she said, "but I hadn't thought of that."

"That would seem to be a logical thing to do," Mason commented, making his voice elaborately casual. "If he accused you of murder he would have to have a corpse. Whereas, if he accused you of embezzlement he would only have to swear that a large sum of money was missing."

"Yes," she said, and then added slowly, "I see your point."

"And just what did you have in mind?" Mason asked.

"I wanted to give you a retainer and have it so that

you'd be willing to act as my attorney, to come to my rescue in case I should telephone. . . . No matter what it was I wanted."

"How much of a retainer did you have in mind?" Mason asked.

"Would three hundred dollars do?"

"I would say that that would be a reasonable retainer," Mason said. "Of course, after you consulted me and in case the situation became complicated, I'd have to ask for more money."

She opened her hand purse, held it carefully so that Mason could not see the contents, and took out six fifty-dollar bills.

"Do I give them to you or give them to your bookkeeper?" she asked.

"My secretary will make a receipt," Mason said. ". . . Those fifty-dollar bills look uniformly crisp."

Her laugh was nervous. "Well, I prepared myself. I don't ordinarily carry large sums of money like this. I got these for you—at my bank."

"Here in the city?" Mason asked quite casually with a quick glance at Della Street.

"No, no, not here in the city. Heavens, no."

"I see," Mason said, picking up the fifty-dollar bills and fingering them casually.

"Just what did you expect me to do for you?" he asked.

"Probably nothing. Don't misunderstand me, Mr. Mason. You are just an anchor out to windward. If all goes well you'll never hear from me again. I'll walk out of this office and out of your life."

"And if all doesn't go well?" Mason asked.

"Then you'll hear from me."

"And what will I hear?"

"I don't know. I'll be calling on you for help."

"What sort of help?"

"I don't know, perhaps advice in a tight situation."

"I can't establish a relationship with a client on that kind of a basis," Mason said.

"You mean financially?"

"In part."

"At the time I call on you for help we'll discuss additional fees. I know that you'll be fair with me and I certainly won't ask you to do anything which is unfair, inequitable or unjust."

"Or illegal?" Mason asked, with a twinkle in his eye.

She started to say "or illegal" but suddenly caught herself, hesitated a moment, then said, "You wouldn't do anything that was illegal, so why waste time talking about it?"

"Then you'll get in touch with me if you need me?"

"Very definitely."

Mason said, "You can reach me at this office during office hours. During the evening you can reach me through the Drake Detective Agency, which has an office on the same floor here in this building."

"I saw the sign on the door as I walked down from the elevator," she said.

"They have a twenty-four-hour switchboard," Mason said, "and in the event of any emergency—that is, if it's a *real* emergency—they can usually get in touch with me."

Della Street handed her a card. "Here are the numbers," she said, "day and night."

"Thank you, Miss Street."

Mason said to Della, "Make out a receipt, Della, for a three-hundred-dollar retainer in the form of cash. Now, do you want this made simply to the Code Number thirty-six, twenty-four, thirty-six?"

She shook her head. "I don't want any receipt." She slipped the loop of her purse over her wrist, picked up the black cosmetics bag, smiled at Della Street, said, "Thank you for seeing me, Mr. Mason," and walked out.

Mason sat watching the automatic doorstop as it closed the door.

When the latch had clicked, Mason said to Della, "You know she put on a good act."

"In what way?"

"That we'd never see her again."

"You think it was an act?"

"I'll give you ten to one," Mason said, "that within a matter of five days that girl calls us up and is in serious difficulties—difficulties which she has already anticipated."

"No takers," Della said. "It's bad luck to take the other side of a bet with you. I'll tell you one thing, however, those weren't *her* measurements. She's nearer thirty-two, twenty-four, thirty-six."

Mason thought that over. "Padding?" he asked.

"Not that much," Della said. "She's using quite a bit, but not that much."

"Now that you mention it, Della," Mason said, "I see

what you mean. So we have a client who is lying to us right at the start."

"Sailing under *false* colors," Della Street said, smiling.

Mason said meditatively, " 'The Case of the Falsified Tape.' "

"Let's hope it doesn't turn out to be 'The Case of the Costly Client,' " Della said. "I'm suspicious of padded stories, padded expense accounts, and padded clients."

"She sneaked up on my blind side," Mason said. "I should have given her more of a third degree and broken down her story. However, it's too late now. We'll ride along with her false measurements."

Chapter Two

AT TEN MINUTES after nine Mason entered his private office through the hall door, smiled a greeting at Della Street, said, "Anybody in the outer office, Della?"

She shook her head and then said, "Gertie."

"Well, Gertie is supposed to be there."

"Gertie's there, hitting on all six," Della said. "Gertie is so excited she is running around in circles."

"What's excited Gertie?"

"Your mysterious client of yesterday."

Mason's eyebrows rose in surprise. "We've heard from her again?"

"Gertie has."

"What do you mean?"

Della motioned to Mason's desk. On top of the mail was a folded newspaper, opened at the section of CLASSIFIED ADS and folded so that the so-called "Personals" were on top.

Mason walked over to the desk, seated himself in the cushioned swivel chair, picked up the paper, let his eyes glance down the section of personal columns, and noticed the ad which had been marked in the margin:

AM HERE READY TO CONCLUDE NEGOTIATIONS ON STRAIGHT CASH BASIS. NO CHECKS. SPOT CASH. CONTACT ME AT WILLATSON HOTEL. 36-24-36.

"Well, I'll be darned," Mason said. "Do you suppose that's our gal?"

"Sounds like it," Della said.

"Hang it," Mason said, "that's what comes of taking a case sight-unseen. Now, that gal is mixed up in some adventure which is going to get her into trouble just as sure as shooting. And when she gets into trouble she's going to look to us to get her out."

Mason hesitated a moment, then jerked his thumb toward the telephone. "Paul Drake, Della."

Della dialed Paul Drake's unlisted number and, in a moment, said, "Just a minute, Paul, Perry wants to talk with you."

She handed the phone over to Mason.

"Hi, Paul," Mason said, "are you too busy to come down to the office for a minute?"

"Never too busy but what the scent of new business causes me to come running!"

"Come running, then," Mason said, and hung up.

Della Street said, "Is it ethical for you to tell Paul. . . ?"

"It isn't ethical for me to tell him anything," Mason said, "not at this stage of the game—at least the way I interpret ethics. But I'm going to find out something about who this gal is seeing and what it's all about."

"Any idea?" Della asked.

Mason said, "I think she came down from San Francisco."

"Why?"

"The way she's dressed for one thing," Mason said, "plus the time of day she came in. She took a plane down, checked her baggage somewhere, probably at the Willatson Hotel, took a cab, came up here. . . . And she had probably arranged to put that ad in the paper before she ever came down here. As I remember it, it takes a day or two to get an ad of that sort published. . . . If that's correct, she telephoned the Willatson Hotel for a reservation."

"And so?" Della asked.

"And so," Mason said, "we're going to find out a little bit about our mysterious client, a little bit more than the three measurements."

Paul Drake's code knock sounded on the corridor door of the private office. Della opened the door. "Hi, Paul," she said. "How's the digestive system?"

"Better, thanks, Beautiful. You folks haven't had me sitting up all night on cases where I've had to eat soggy hamburgers at an office desk. I've dined out on good, freshly cooked meat now for six days in succession."

"Business that bad?" Mason asked.

"Lousy," Drake said.

"Maybe we can help," Mason told him. "But this isn't a big case, it's just a routine job."

"Who's the client?" Drake asked.

"I am," Mason said.

"Oh, oh."

"He wants to find out about a client," Della said.

Drake settled himself in the overstuffed leather chair, threw his legs over the rounded arm, took out a note-book and a fountain pen, and said, "Shoot."

Mason said, "I think I let a client down, Paul."

"How come?"

Mason hesitated, spoke cautiously. "I can't tell you the details without violating the code of ethics, Paul. An attorney is supposed to protect the confidences of his client. Any statements that are made are completely confidential.

"Now then, with that in mind I want you to know that I am afraid I gave a client advice which fell short of the advice I should have given."

"Male or female?" Drake asked.

"That also is confidential," Mason said.

"Well, how did you fail this client?"

"I didn't tell the client the things the client should have known for the client's own good," Mason said. "I let the client diagnose the case and accepted that diagnosis."

"How come?"

Mason said, "Every once in a while a client wants to diagnose the case, just as a patient will come to a doctor and say, 'Doctor, I have indigestion. I want you to give me something for indigestion.'

"If the doctor simply gives the patient something for indigestion he is untrue to his profession.

"What the doctor should do is ask about symptoms

connected with the indigestion. He finds out that the patient has been having pains in the chest and occasionally down the left arm, so he suspects something entirely different from indigestion. He has a cardiograph made and finds out that the patient is suffering from a high cholesterol count. He doesn't give the patient medicine for indigestion, but puts the patient on a diet consisting of no fats, no dairy foods, but high in proteins.

"The patient gets better.

"If, on the other hand, the doctor had accepted the patient's self-diagnosis, the patient would probably have been dead inside of twelve months."

"That," Drake said, "is rather elementary, isn't it, Perry?"

"I'm making it elementary," Mason explained, "because I want to show you the situation.

"This client came here and diagnosed the case and prescribed the remedy. Unfortunately, I accepted the statements at face value. I shouldn't have done that. Now then, in order to appease my own conscience, I want information."

"About the client?" Drake asked.

"About various and sundry things," Mason said. "They do not necessarily have any *direct* bearing on the situation. They may not even *directly* concern the client. But they are sufficiently significant so they concern me."

"All right," Drake said, "you've now reached your thumb by going all the way around your elbow. You want me to do a job. It's a job in which you are the

client. You'll get the best service I can give and you'll
get a discount on the bill. What do I do?"

Mason took the folded newspaper and handed it to
Drake.

"That ad," he said.

Drake read the ad aloud:

"AM HERE READY TO CONCLUDE NEGOTIATIONS
ON STRAIGHT CASH BASIS. NO CHECKS.
SPOT CASH. CONTACT ME AT WILLATSON
HOTEL. 36-24-36."

Drake looked up from the newspaper. "That's the
ad that interests you?"

Mason nodded.

"Your party evidently has three rooms," Drake said.
. . . "No, wait a minute, thirty-six is mentioned twice.
It may be two rooms, thirty-six and twenty-four, and
then the person putting in the ad signs it thirty-six to
show that that's the room where contact is to be made."

"Could be," Mason said.

Drake regarded him shrewdly. "And it could be some
sort of a code," he said.

Mason was silent.

"Exactly what is it you want me to do?" the detective
inquired.

"Find out everything you can about who put that
ad in the paper and the person for whom the message
was intended."

Drake said, "That may be a big job, or it may be
rather simple. The Willatson Hotel is a commercial-

type hotel. When there are conventions in town it's probably about ninety-five percent occupied. At other times the percentage of occupancy may be sixty to seventy percent. In any event there will be too many people just to go at it blind. I can find out who's in room thirty-six and who's in room twenty-four. That may not mean anything.

"The best bet is to try to get a line on whoever put the ad in the paper by making a dummy reply in the press, saying something like:

"MESSAGE NOT CLEAR. YOU CAN REACH ME
TELEPHONE NUMBER 676-2211 TO CLARIFY.
AM NOT WALKING INTO ANY TRAP REGARDLESS
OF TYPE OF BAIT USED."

Drake made a little gesture and said, "Of course, that's just off the top of my head, Perry. I'd have to word it a little more carefully than that. I'd have to be subtle, but even so the chances are that there'd be some false note in the reply which would alarm the quarry and let your client know that some outsider was checking."

"Well," Mason said thoughtfully, "I don't know as there's any reason why a situation of that sort should be fatal. . . . It might send the client back to me and then I could . . ." His voice trailed away into silence.

"What's the matter?" Drake asked. "Can't you phone your client at the Willatson Hotel and—"

"I didn't say I thought the person who put this ad in was my client," Mason said. "The client may well be the one to whom the ad is addressed."

"In other words, you don't know where to reach your client?"

"Come, come," Mason said, "you haven't been reading your decisions of the Supreme Court lately. Before I can be questioned I have to be advised of my constitutional rights and given an opportunity to consult a lawyer. . . . I've given you a job to do. Get busy and do it."

Drake thought for a moment and said, "This situation has overtones which intrigue the hell out of me, Perry, but, after all, you said it, you've given me a job to do. It's up to me to get busy."

Drake heaved himself up out of the chair. "When do you want reports?" he asked.

"As soon as you have something definite to report. No matter how trivial it seems to you, give me a line on it."

"Day and night?" Drake asked.

"It's not exactly *that* urgent," Mason said. "Let's say day and evening."

"Okay," Drake said, "day and evening it is. Any limit as to the number of people I can put on it?"

"Don't go over five hundred dollars until you have asked me," Mason said.

"With your discount," Drake told him, "you can get quite a bit of investigative work done for five hundred bucks. . . . I'll be in touch, Perry."

Mason and Della Street watched the detective out the door. Then Mason heaved a sigh, picked up the pile of papers on his desk, and said, "Well, Della, we've done all *we* can do. I guess now we'll get to work."

"How are we going to enter this on the books?" Della asked. "You take in three hundred dollars, you pay out five hundred, and we don't even have a name for the client in the case."

"Call her Miss Deficit then," Mason said. "That will serve until we have a better name."

"Perhaps," Della mused, "it could be Miss Deceit."

"She hasn't deceived us," Mason said. "At least we don't know that she has. What we need is information. She has diagnosed her own case, prescribed her own remedy, and she may be wrong on both counts."

Della Street picked up her shorthand notebook and pencil. "Well," she observed, "we're only starting the day two hundred dollars worse off than when you sat down at the desk."

Chapter Three

THE NEXT DAY Perry Mason was in court all day defending a young Negro lad who had been accused of robbing a pawnshop.

The identification by three eyewitnesses who had seen the robber running madly down the street, jumping into a parked car, and making off at high speed was absolutely positive.

In vain Mason tried to shake the identification of the witnesses.

At three o'clock the Deputy District Attorney concluded his opening argument and Mason had an opportunity to address the jury.

"Contrary to popular belief, gentlemen, circumstantial evidence is about the strongest we have, and eyewitness evidence is about the weakest.

"Here is a tall, young Negro lad with a mustache, carrying a paper bag.

"The place in question was held up by a tall, young Negro lad, wearing a mustache, carrying a paper bag.

"It is the theory of the prosecution that the defendant made his escape, hid the money somewhere, put half a dozen packages of cigarettes in the paper bag, and then, when he was arrested, explained that he had been running short of cigarettes; that he went to a coin-vending machine in the neighborhood, bought the six packages of cigarettes, put them in a paper bag he had taken with him, and was returning to his modest apartment when he was apprehended by the police.

"I ask you, if he had disposed of the money so that he could conceal the evidence against him, why, in the name of reason, didn't he also dispose of the paper bag?

"A tall, young Negro with a mustache and carrying a paper bag was like a magnet to the police within a matter of minutes after the holdup when the alarm had been broadcast on an all-points bulletin.

"People get a fleeting glimpse of an individual. They remember the salient points. In this case, that he was a tall, young Negro with a paper bag and a mustache. That is all they really remember.

"Later on when they try to cudgel their recollection into producing additional facts at the insistence of the police officers, they hypnotize themselves into believing there are other things which they remember clearly. Later on they are given photographs to look at, the so-called mug shots of the police. They are asked to study these photographs carefully. They study them until they see the defendant in a line-up and promptly pick him out as the man they saw running down the street, carrying a paper bag.

"It is a case of self-hypnotism.

"It is incumbent upon the prosecution to prove its case beyond all reasonable doubt. I ask you to return a verdict of not guilty."

Mason returned to his seat.

The Deputy District Attorney in his closing argument resorted to sarcasm.

"The defendant robs the store. He puts the money in a paper bag. He is seen running down the street by three witnesses. He tries to fabricate the evidence after he has hidden the money by putting some packages of cigarettes in the paper bag so that it will look like an entirely innocent transaction.

"Three reputable eyewitnesses identify this man positively. Perry Mason, who is one of the shrewdest cross-examiners in the country, has resorted to every arrow in his legal quiver to weaken the testimony of these men. They remain unshaken.

"Don't be hypnotized by eloquence. Don't by swayed by spurious reasoning. Don't be conned out of your just convictions. Go out and find this man guilty."

It was after five o'clock by the time the Judge had finished his instructions, and the jury retired immediately.

It was expected there would be a quick verdict, but the jury was taken out to dinner at six-thirty, returned at eight, and resumed deliberations. By nine o'clock the buzzer sounded and the jury announced they had agreed upon a verdict.

The courthouse grapevine promptly transmitted the news.

The jury had found the defendant guilty.

The Judge took his place on the bench, the defendant was brought into court. All was in readiness for the jury to be received when a plain-clothes officer hurriedly pushed his way through the swinging doors of the courtroom, dashed down the central aisle, approached the bench, and said something in a whisper to the Judge.

The Judge frowned, leaned forward for a whispered colloquy. Then the Court said to the bailiff, "You will keep the jury waiting for a few minutes. I will ask counsel for both sides to join me in chambers."

When the Judge had retired to chambers, he kept on his judicial robes, seated himself in the creaking swivel chair back of his desk, and said, "Gentlemen, there has been a surprising development in this case.

"The police have apprehended a man in the act of holding up a store. They found a cache of money containing one of the hundred-dollar bills taken from the store in the robbery which is being presently tried before this court.

"You gentlemen will remember that the proprietor had taken the numbers of those hundred-dollar bills. The culprit has confessed to the holdup. It appears that the defendant in this case is innocent."

"What!" the Deputy District Attorney exclaimed.

The Judge nodded.

"But they've agreed on a verdict," the prosecutor blurted. "It's 'guilty.' "

"We can't let that verdict be received in court," the Judge said, "and there is a legal point. Having agreed upon the verdict, I don't know offhand exactly what the legal status of the case is. I could, of course, call the jury into court, explain the circumstances to them, and instruct them to return a verdict of 'not guilty'. But it is my present idea that the best thing to do is to tell the jury that circumstances have occurred which necessitate their discharge before any verdict is formally received in court."

"Explaining the circumstances to them, of course," Mason said.

"Certainly not!" the Deputy District Attorney objected.

"Why not?" the Judged asked.

"Because this would tend to weaken the whole fabric of identification evidence," the Deputy protested.

"Otherwise," Mason said, "the twelve people on that jury are going out and criticize the Judge and the administration of justice. It's a lot better to have the people lose a little faith in too confident, too cocksure eyewitness identification than it is to lose confidence in the administration of justice."

"I think so, too," the Judge said, pushing back his swivel chair and getting to his feet.

"Gentlemen, we will return to court. I will call the jury in, and before I ask them if they have agreed upon a verdict, I will make a brief statement to them advising them of recent developments and discharge the jury. At that time you, Mr. Deputy District Attorney, can ask for a motion dismissing the case. It will be granted."

The Deputy District Attorney accepted the Judge's decision with poor grace. They returned to the courtroom, and the Judge made a brief statement to the jurors as to what had happened.

Mason enjoyed watching their astounded expressions as they realized the significance of what the Judge was saying.

Then the lawyer shook hands with the jurors. The jurors, after some hesitancy, shook hands with the defendant, and Mason said to his client, "Go home and shave that mustache off and never wear one again. Also never carry a paper bag."

The defendant laughed. "Tall Negro boy with a mustache. Tall Negro boy with a paper bag, yes, *sir*. I am going back home and shave off that mustache just as soon as I can get my hands on a razor, and I'm *never* going to carry anything in a paper bag again!"

Mason, tired after the long trial, nevertheless stopped in at his office on the way home.

Della Street had left a note for him:

8:45 P.M. COULDN'T WAIT ANY LONGER,
  BUT WANTED YOU TO SEE THE AD IN THE
  EVENING PAPER. IT'S ON YOUR DESK.

Mason picked up the folded paper, looked at the ad which had been circled.

The ad read:

36-24-36. WANT TO AVOID ANY TRAPS.
WILL BE AT HOTEL ENTRANCE IN TAXICAB
AT EXACTLY NINE O'CLOCK TONIGHT.
CONTACT ME THERE. NO WITNESSES,
PLEASE. U NO HOO.

Mason regarded the ad thoughtfully, then dialed the number of the Drake Detective Agency.

"Perry Mason talking," he said. "Is Paul Drake in?"

"No, he isn't. Mr. Drake's out working on a case. He said he didn't know when he'd be back."

"Anyone there know what job he's working on?" Mason asked.

"I'm afraid not," the secretary said. "Mr. Drake said it was extremely confidential."

"Thank you," Mason said. "I guess that's all we can do tonight."

The lawyer hung up the phone, closed the office, went to his apartment, and sank into deep sleep.

Chapter Four

PAUL DRAKE was already at his office at nine o'clock the next morning when Perry Mason, leaving the elevator, detoured into the office of the Drake Detective Agency.

The girl at the switchboard smiled, nodded, pointed down the corridor toward Drake's private office, and returned to the telephone conversation she was holding at the switchboard.

Mason walked down a veritable rabbit warren of cubbyhole offices where Drake's operatives prepared reports on their various cases, and then entered Drake's personal office at the end of the passageway.

This also was a tiny office with a desk and a battery of telephones.

Drake looked up at Mason, grinned, yawned, said, "You and your mysterious client!"

"How come?" Mason asked.

Drake passed him over the newspaper containing the ad which Della Street had left on his desk the night before.

"Some of your work?" the lawyer asked.

"My work," Drake admitted.

"Do any good with it?"

"Yes and no."

"What happened?"

"Well, I had to take certain chances—that's one of the things you have to figure on in this game. I'm playing it blind. The other side has all the numbers.

"Now, either this party had already contacted the person she wanted, or she hadn't. I couldn't tell which."

"Wait a minute," Mason said. "You're using a female pronoun. Why?"

"Because she is a female."

"Go on."

"Well, as I said, either she had contacted the person or she hadn't. Then I had another horn of the dilemma. Either she knew the person by sight or she didn't. The fact that she put that ad in the paper indicated the probabilities were that she didn't know the party by sight.

"Of course, I had one other chance to take. Either the party was a man or a woman. I was in a position to hedge a little bit on that by taking one of my women operatives with me.

"I put that ad in the paper, stating that I would be parked in front of the hotel entrance in a taxicab at exactly nine o'clock."

Mason said, "I presume you had made other efforts to find her identity?"

"Of course. I went to the office of the newspaper which had run her ad. A five-dollar bill got me the information that she was a young woman, good figure, blond, blue eyes, a little bit diffident.

"I went to the Willatson Hotel and wasted five dollars. I couldn't get any lead there.

"So I decided to take a chance and put this ad in the paper. Then, with my female operative, I went to the hotel and sat in front in a taxicab."

"Why the taxicab?" Mason asked.

"So she couldn't trace the license number."

Mason nodded approvingly. "What happened?"

"Promptly at nine o'clock she walked past the car, but so did a lot of other people. However, I had it fixed so she couldn't get a real good look at either my female operative or myself. I was wearing a cap pulled down over my forehead and dark glasses. The operative was wearing a coat with a high collar and dark glasses. . . . It was all real cloak-and-dagger.

"With all those people walking past we couldn't spot her the first time, but when she turned at the end of the block and walked back we had her spotted. She did that three times, never giving us the faintest tumble; no signal, no recognition, no attempt to come up and engage us in conversation. She just walked past four times. And she was clever enough so she didn't indicate any particular curiosity. She kept her eyes straight ahead each time she passed the cab."

"And so?" Mason asked.

"So," Drake said, "we didn't press our luck. We had the cab drive away."

"You didn't try to shadow her?"

"Of course, we shadowed her. I had one operative in

an automobile parked behind me, and when the girl walked past the cab the second time he spotted her the same way we did. When we moved on I gave him the signal to follow her.

"After our cab drove off she went back to the Willatson Hotel. She's registered as Miss Diana Deering of San Francisco. She's in room seven-sixty-seven."

"Good work, Paul," Mason said.

"Wait a minute," Drake told him, "I'm not finished. We put some more five-dollar bills to work with the bellboys and the phone operator. Her luggage is stamped D.D.

"Now, when a person assumes an alias they quite frequently use their own first name, and, of course, with initials on the baggage they want to get a name that tallies with the initials. So Diana Deering could well be Diana——, of San Francisco."

Mason raised his eyebrows.

"So," Drake went on, "we did a little leg work. We found that our subject telephoned a San Francisco hospital from time to time to inquire about a patient, one Edgar Douglas.

"Edgar is employed by the Escobar Import and Export Company of San Francisco. He was in an automobile accident a few days ago, has a fractured skull, and is still unconscious.

"So we took the initials of Diana D. and tried Douglas as the last name. We phoned the Escobar Company and asked about Edgar Douglas, were told about the automobile accident, and asked about Diana Douglas.

"We were told she was his sister, that she was also an employee of the company, was upset about the accident, and had been given a leave of absence for a few days so she could be near him.

"We got a description. It checks. We also found out there are no other members of the family."

"Arouse any suspicion?" Mason asked.

"Not a bit. We said we were a finance company checking on Edgar's employment and credit standing, made the questions as routine as possible and asked them in a somewhat bored tone of voice."

"Then what?" Mason asked.

"So then we did leg work in San Francisco," Drake went on. "The Escobar Company doesn't seem at all alarmed, but they're having a *'routine'* audit of their books. We found that out more or less incidentally."

"What's the prognosis on the brother?" Mason asked.

"Probably going to be all right, but may be unconscious for as much as two weeks," Drake said. "The guy was all set to take a business trip somewhere—that is, suitcase all packed; drove to a service station to get the car filled up; was clobbered by a car which drove through a red light and knocked him unconscious."

"Any question that it was his fault?" Mason asked.

"None whatever. Not only did the car that struck him come through a red light with several witnesses willing to testify to that effect, but the driver was pretty well potted. The police took him to jail to sober up and he's facing a citation for drunk driving."

Mason was thoughtful for several seconds. "Why

should all this cause Diana to leave her brother, critically ill, come to Los Angeles, and start putting ads in the paper?"

Drake shrugged his shoulders and said, "If you want us to keep on we'll find out. Probably it's some form of blackmail which involves the family in some way."

"You say there are no other members of the family?" Mason asked.

"That's all. The parents are dead. Diana and her brother, Edgar, are the only survivors at the present time. Diana has never been married. Edgar is a bachelor, but the rumor is he's going to announce an engagement to a wealthy heiress—although that's just rumor."

"How old?" Mason asked.

"Diana?"

"No, Edgar."

"A little over twenty-one."

"Younger than Diana," Mason said thoughtfully.

"A couple of years."

"She could try to mother him a little," Mason said.

"It has been done," Drake conceded. . . . "How about you giving a helping hand?"

"To whom?"

"To me, and, incidentally, to yourself," Drake said. "If you can tell me about Diana's case and why you're interested I may be able to help both of you. At least I can save you a little money."

Mason shook his head. "I can't, Paul. I'm bound by professional ethics."

"Do you want me to keep on the job?" Drake asked.

"For a while," Mason said.

"Want me to put a tail on her?"

Mason said, "I'd like to know where she goes and who she sees, but that's a pretty ticklish job because I don't want her to feel that she's being shadowed. If that happened it might alarm her and cause her to take steps which would be against her own best interests."

Drake said, "Then you'd better let me make a very casual shadow job of it, because on a tight shadow job the subject is quite frequently aware of the tail. It's a pretty difficult job to put on a real shadow and guarantee that the subject is completely unaware of it."

"Then make it a loose shadow job," Mason said.

"Of course," Drake went on, "where money is no object, we can use enough operatives to—"

"We haven't an unlimited expense account here, Paul, and I don't know that it's absolutely imperative that we know where this young woman goes and what she does, but I would like to keep in touch with her and I would dislike very, very much to have her become alarmed and take a powder."

"Okay," Drake said, "I'll see what can be done. We'll make a loose tail job of it. When do you want a report?"

"Whenever you have anything worthwhile," Mason said, put his hand briefly on Paul Drake's shoulder, and walked down to his own office.

Chapter Five

THE WILLATSON HOTEL was a commercial hotel which operated on a basis of live-and-let-live. Very little attention was paid to people who came through the doors, crossed the lobby, and walked directly to the elevator.

Perry Mason, however, felt it better to follow the procedure of being a total stranger.

He went to the desk, caught the eye of the clerk, and said, "Do you have a Miss Diana Deering registered here?"

"Just a moment."

The clerk looked through a file and said, "Seven-sixty-seven."

"Will you announce me, please?"

The clerk seemed bored. "What name?"

"She won't know the name," Mason said. "It's in connection with a social-security inquiry. Tell her it has to do with thirty-six, dash, twenty-four, dash, thirty-six."

The clerk said, "Very well," picked up the phone,

rang Room 767, and said, "A gentleman is here to see you in connection with an inquiry about a number. I believe it's a social-security number. . . . What's that? . . . Very well, I'll tell him if that's your message."

He turned to Mason, said, "She is having no social-security problems. You'll have to give me a name or—"

Mason raised his voice and said, "You didn't give her the number: thirty-six, twenty-four, thirty-six."

The receiver suddenly made squawking sounds.

The clerk said, "It's quite all right. She wants to see you. She heard you give the number over the telephone. You may go on up."

The clerk hung up the telephone and returned to the task of bookkeeping with a manner of bored indifference.

Mason took the elevator to the seventh floor and knocked on the door of Room 767.

The young woman who had been in his office earlier in the week opened the door quickly, then fell back in amazement. "Good heavens!" she exclaimed. "You!"

"Why not?" Mason asked.

"How . . . how did you know where I was? . . . How did you know who I—"

Mason pushed his way into the room as she fell back, closed the door, walked over to a chair, and seated himself.

"Now, let's talk a little sense for a change," he said. "Your real name is Diana?"

"Yes."

"Diana what?"

"Diana Deering."

"Let's try doing better than that," Mason said.

"That's my name, Mr. Mason. You ask down at the desk if you don't believe it. That's—"

"That's the name you're registered under," Mason interrupted. "But that's not your name. How about Diana Douglas of San Francisco? Would that do any better?"

For a moment her eyes showed dismay, then her face flushed. "I retained you as *my* attorney," she said. "You're supposed to help me, not to go chasing around trying to uncover things about my past, trying to cooperate with . . ."

Her voice trailed into silence.

"With the police?" Mason asked.

"No, not with the police," she said. "Thank heavens, I haven't done anything that violates the law."

"Are you sure?"

"Of course I'm sure."

"Look here," Mason said, "I'm an attorney. People come to me when they're in trouble. I'm supposed to help them. You came to me and sneaked up on my blind side. I didn't do a very good job of helping you. I'm sorry about that. That's why I decided I'd better find you before it was too late."

"You're mistaken, Mr. Mason. I'm not in any trouble. I'm trying to—to protect a friend."

"You're in trouble," Mason said. "Does the Escobar Import and Export Company know where you are?"

"I don't know. . . . They know that I'm away on personal business."

Mason reached across her lap, picked up the black handbag.

"You leave that alone!" she screamed, grabbing his arm with both hands.

Mason kept his grip on the bag.

"Full of money?" he asked.

"That's none of your business. I want to fire you right now. I wanted an attorney to protect me. You're worse than the police. Let go of that bag. You're fired!"

"Where did you get the money that's in this bag?" Mason asked.

"That's none of your business!"

"Did you, perhaps, embezzle it from the company where you worked?" the lawyer asked.

"Good heavens, no!"

"You're sure?"

"Of course I'm sure!"

Mason shook his head. "Would it surprise you to know that the Escobar Import and Export Company called in an auditor to go over its books?"

Her face showed surprise, then consternation. Her grip on his arm weakened. "Why, why in the world— good heavens . . . they couldn't."

"That's the information I have," Mason said. "Now, suppose you do a little talking and try telling the truth for a change. What's your capacity with the Escobar Import and Export Company? What do you do?"

"I'm a cashier and bookkeeper. I have charge of foreign exchange and foreign payments. I . . . Mr. Mason, there *must* be some mistake."

Mason said, "Let's look at basic facts. You come to my office. You have a bag that's loaded with money. You—"

"How did you know about what's in this bag?"

"My receptionist had a chance to see the inside of it," Mason said. "It was loaded with bills."

"Oh," she said, and then was silent.

Mason said, "You put an ad in the paper indicating that you were here to pay off a blackmail demand. So, let's put two and two together. You take an assumed name. You come to Los Angeles. You put an ad in the paper. You are dealing with a blackmailer. You have a large sum of money with you in the form of cash. The company where you work evidently feels some money is missing. It calls in an auditor."

Diana sat silent. From the open window came noises of traffic from the street.

"Well?" Mason asked, after a while.

"It's absolutely fantastic," she said, removing her hands from Mason's arm. "There's—there's nothing I can do."

"I'm trying to help you," Mason reminded her. "You've made it rather difficult for me so far. Perhaps if you tried telling me the truth I could put in my time helping you instead of running around in circles trying to cut your back trail. . . . Now, *did* you embezzle that money?"

"Heavens, no!"

"How much money do you have in this bag in the form of cash?"

"Five thousand dollars."

"Where did you get it?"

She was silent for a moment, then said, "I'm going to tell you the truth."

Mason settled back in his chair, said, "You're a little bit late with it and I don't know how much time we have, but go ahead."

She said, "The whole thing happened when my brother was injured in an automobile accident. After they took him to the hospital I went to his room to get some things for him—shaving things and things of that sort that I thought he'd need in the hospital, and I found his bags all packed and a letter addressed simply 'DEAR FUGITIVE.' The letter said that the writer was fed up with waiting around; that either he should receive five thousand dollars by Tuesday night or other action would be taken."

"How was the letter written?" Mason asked.

"In typing. It was all typed, even the signature."

"And the signature was 36-24-36?"

"That's right."

"And the postmark?"

"Los Angeles."

"So, what did you do?"

"Mr. Mason, my brother was unconscious in the hospital. I couldn't let him down. I arranged to put an ad in the paper, just as the letter said I was to do, and came down here."

"And the money?"

"My brother had the money in a briefcase in his

apartment. He was all ready to go. Apparently, he was going to drive down. He had the briefcase with the money, a suitcase and an overnight bag."

"And where did he get the money?"

"Mr. Mason, I . . . I don't know."

"Your brother works in the same company you do?"

"Yes."

"Could he have embezzled the money from the company?"

"Mr. Mason, in the first place Edgar wouldn't ever do anything criminal. In the second place, he wouldn't have had access to the money. The cash is kept in a money safe in the vault. Only the top executives have the combination."

"But you have it?"

"Yes, it's my job to check the books on the cash—not every day, but twice a month I have to add up the withdrawal slips and see that everything balances."

"Tell me a little more about Edgar," Mason said.

"He's young. He's a year and a half younger than I am. He . . . our parents were killed five years ago. I've tried to help Edgar every way I could. He's a sensitive individual who—"

"You're both working for the Escobar Export and Import Company. Who got the job there first?"

"I did."

"What about the company?"

"It engages in exports and imports just as the name indicates."

"What kind of a company?"

"What do you mean?"

"A big company, a little company, a—"

"No, it's pretty much of a one-man concern."

"Who's the big wheel?"

"Mr. Gage—Franklin T. Gage."

"How many employees?"

"Oh, perhaps ten or fifteen altogether. There are five working full time in the office and an auditor and tax man."

"Do I understand then there are others who work outside of the office?"

"Yes, there are scouts and buyers."

"But nevertheless they are employees?"

"In a sense, yes."

"How old a man is Franklin Gage?"

"Forty-something or other. Perhaps forty-five."

"He runs the company?"

"Yes. He's the big shot."

"Who's next in command?"

"Homer."

"Homer Gage?"

"Yes."

"His son?"

"His nephew."

Mason's eyes narrowed thoughtfully. "How long after you started work there did your brother, Edgar, start work?"

"About six months."

"And what was he doing during those six months?"

"He was doing nothing. He had been let out at the

place where he was working. He became involved in a lot of office intrigue and— It's too long a story to tell you."

"Who supported him?"

"So then after six months, you got a job for him there

"I did."

at the company where you work. . . . Who gave him the job, Franklin Gage or Homer?"

"Franklin."

Mason regarded her shrewdly. "You didn't talk to Homer about it?"

"I talked to Mr. Gage. Mr. Franklin Gage."

"At the office?"

"No, I worked late one night and he said that I'd missed my dinner on account of working and that the company was going to buy my dinner."

"So in the intimacy of that little dinner party you took occasion to tell him about your brother and asked him if Edgar could have a job?"

"Yes. Only you make it sound so very . . . so very calculating."

Mason brushed her remark aside with a wave of his hand. "How did Homer react to that?"

"I didn't ask Homer."

"That wasn't my question," Mason answered. "I wanted to know how Homer reacted to it."

"Well," she said, "I think that Homer felt that we really didn't need to take on Edgar at the time."

"And what are Edgar's duties? What does he do?"

"He's a liaison man."

"Now then," Mason went on, "Edgar had been out of

work for six months and you had been supporting him?"

"I'd been helping out. He had unemployment insurance and—"

"So where," Mason interrupted, "did he get five thousand dollars in cash?"

"I—I just don't know."

"Not from you?"

"No."

"Do you have five thousand dollars?"

"I . . . yes, I do."

"More than that?"

"A very little more."

"Where is it?"

"In savings banks."

Mason took mental inventory of the situation, then said abruptly, "This Homer Gage, what's his attitude toward you?"

"Friendly."

"Very friendly?" Mason asked.

"I think he'd like to be."

"Married or single?"

"Married."

"Ever met his wife?"

"Not formally. She's been at the office a couple of times to get checks cashed or something like that. She's smart-looking . . . you know, very much on the ball. They say she's a bitch."

"Her husband steps out?"

"I wouldn't know. I do know his married life isn't happy."

"You see him looking at the other girls in the office.

Doubtless you've discussed him with the other girls.
Does he keep them after hours?"

"I don't know. I think perhaps . . . well, I just don't
know."

"Does he step out?"

"I told you I wouldn't know."

"Does he step out?"

"All right, if you're going to be insistent about it, I
think he does, but I wouldn't know."

"And Homer's had you stay after hours more than
once?"

She hesitated, then said, in a low voice, "Yes." Then
added quickly, "You see the business is very, very un-
conventional. It's a complicated deal of buying and selling in large lots, and quite frequently the deals are
made on a spot-cash basis.

"This is particularly true in connection with Oriental
goods. You see, we have to have a Certificate of Origin on
goods which are taken out of Hong Kong, for instance,
and . . . well, sometimes matters have to be handled
with a great deal of diplomacy."

"So sometimes you work late?"

"Yes."

"And Homer has had you work late?"

"Yes."

"And taken you out to dinner?"

"Twice."

"And propositioned you?"

"What do you mean by that, Mr. Mason?"

"You know what I mean."

"If you mean has he ever come out cold turkey with

a proposition, the answer is 'no', but all men proposition you. They size you up. They look you over. They make a remark occasionally with a double meaning. They tell a story that's a little broad. They are quick to follow up any opening. . . . Mr. Mason, I don't need to tell you how men are. They're always on the lookout in an aggressive way, and if they get an opening they follow up and just keep pushing."

"And Homer Gage has been like that?"

"He's been like that. He isn't going to come right out in the open and make any proposition and get rebuffed and perhaps have his uncle know what is happening and—"

"The uncle likes you?" Mason said.

"Yes, he does."

"Married or single?"

"He's a widower."

"And how about him? Does he have the aggressive, masculine mannerisms?"

"No, no, Mr. Mason. Mr. Franklin Gage is very much of a gentleman. He is courteous and considerate and—well, he's an older, more mature man and his attitude is . . ."

"Fatherly?" Mason ventured, as she hesitated.

"Well, not exactly fatherly. More like an uncle or something of that sort."

"But he likes you?"

"I think so."

"Very much?"

"I think so. You see, I am pretty good at adjusting myself in a business way and I have tried to do a good job there at the export and import. And Mr. Gage, Mr. Franklin Gage, knows it.

"In a quiet way he's very nice to—to all of the girls who work in the office "

"How many other than you?"

"Three."

"Names?"

"Helen Albert, a stenographer; Joyce Baffin, a secretary-stenographer, but her duties are mostly of a secretarial nature—for Homer Gage; and Ellen Candler, who has charge of the mail and the files."

"Suppose a person wanted to embezzle money from the company?" Mason said. "Would it be easy?"

"Very easy—too easy for those who had the combination to the cash safe. The company keeps large sums of money on hand. Occasionally it's necessary to make deals on a completely cash basis with no voucher of any kind."

"Bribery?" Mason asked.

"I don't think so."

"Smuggling?"

"I don't think it's anything like that."

"And how do you keep your books under those circumstances?" Mason asked.

"Well, there's a certain amount of juggling with the cash so that the books are regular, but sometimes there are transactions which—well, it would be a little difficult to trace them."

"So your brother could very easily have embezzled five thousand dollars to go to Los Angeles and pay off a blackmailer?"

"Mr. Mason, I tell you Edgar wouldn't do that, and even if he had wanted to he couldn't have done it. He doesn't have the combination to the cash safe."

"Who does have the combination?"

"Franklin Gage, Homer Gage, Stewart Garland, our income-tax man, and myself."

"You found five thousand dollars in cash in Edgar's apartment?"

"Yes. I've told you that two or three times. It's the truth."

"And you knew Edgar hadn't had an opportunity to save that much out of his salary since he'd started work?"

"Well, yes."

"Where did you think he got it?"

She said, "My brother is—well, he has friends. He's very likable, very magnetic, and I think he has friends who would help him out in a situation of that sort. . . . That's what I thought."

"All right," Mason said, "let's face it. You're in a jam. You've come to Los Angeles under an assumed name. You've got five thousand dollars in cash. You're mixed up with a blackmailer. Suppose the accounts at the Escobar Import and Export Company show a five-thousand-dollar deficit?"

Her hand went to her throat.

"Now, you're getting the point," Mason told her. "There's only one thing for you to do. Get a plane back to San Francisco. Get into your office tomorrow morning.

"Now, do exactly as I say. If it turns out an auditor says there's a five-thousand-dollar shortage, just laugh

and say, 'Oh, no, there isn't.' Tell the auditor that your
brother was working on a company deal at the time of
the accident; that you took out five thousand dollars to
finance that deal; that Edgar asked you not to make an
entry until he had had a chance to discuss the deal with
Franklin Gage; that he thought it was going to be a
good deal for the company but that you knew all about
the five thousand dollars that he had and knew that it
was company money.

"You go to a local bank this afternoon, deposit the
five thousand, buy a cashier's check payable to you as
trustee. As soon as your brother recovers consciousness,
you'll see him before anyone else does. . . . Make certain of that. As a member of the family you'll have the
right-of-way.

"Then you can use your own judgment."

"But, Mr. Mason, this thing is coming to a head. It
isn't going to wait. This blackmailer—or whatever it is
—this letter that my brother had was most urgent, imperative, demanding."

"What did you do with that letter?"

"I burned it."

Mason said, "There was an ad in the paper for you to
make contact with a cab passenger at—"

"Heavens, how did you know about that?" she asked.

"We make it a point to read the personal ads," Mason said. "Why didn't you contact the man in the taxicab?"

"Because I didn't like the looks of the thing. There
were two passengers, a man and a woman. It was night,

yet they both were wearing dark glasses. I thought it was a trap of some kind. I . . . well, I decided to pass it up. When I made contact I wanted it to be where there were no witnesses."

"I see," Mason said thoughtfully, then abruptly he walked over to the telephone, asked the switchboard operator for an outside line, and got Paul Drake's office.

"Paul," he said, "I want a female operative—blonde, twenty-two, twenty-three, or twenty-four, with a good figure—to come to the Willatson Hotel and go to Room Seven-sixty-seven.

"She can't carry anything with her except a handbag. She can make purchases and have them sent in from the department stores where she buys. She'll take the name of Diana Deering, which is the name of the present occupant of the room."

"I know," Drake said.

"She'll masquerade as Diana Deering. She'll make it a point to get acquainted with the bellboys, with the clerks as they come on duty. She can ask them questions. Inquire about a monthly rate on the room. Do anything which will attract attention to herself as Diana Deering. And quit tailing the real Diana."

Drake said, "It happens that I have a girl who fits the description in the office right now, Perry. She's Stella Grimes. She's worked on one of your cases before, although I don't know if you've seen her personally. The only thing is she's a little older."

"How much older?" Mason asked.

"Tut, tut," Drake said, "you're asking questions."

"You think she can get by?"

"I think she can get by," Drake said.

"Get her up here," Mason told him.

"But what about me?" Diana asked when Mason hung up.

"You're going to get that cashier's check payable to you as trustee and then go back to San Francisco."

"And what about my baggage?"

"You'll have to wait for that."

"How will I get it out of the hotel? Don't they check people when you leave with baggage?"

"Sure they do," Mason said, "but we'll fix that."

"How?"

"I'll rent a room here in the hotel. I'll try to get one on the same floor. We'll move your baggage into that room. Then I'll check out, carrying the baggage with me, go right to the desk, and pay the bill on that room. They'll have no way of knowing that one of the suitcases I'll have with me was taken from Room Seven-sixty-seven."

"And what about this girl who is going to masquerade as me?"

"She'll deal with the blackmailer."

"And if I've turned the money in for a cashier's check, what will we pay him—or her?"

"We won't," Mason said. "It's against the policy of the office to pay blackmailers."

"But what are you going to do? How can you avoid payment?"

"I don't know," Mason told her. "We'll play it by ear. I wish to hell your brother would regain consciousness so we could find out what it's all about. . . . Get your suitcase packed."

Tears came to her eyes. "Edgar's a wonderful boy, Mr. Mason."

Mason said, "I'm going down to a baggage store and get a suitcase. I'll stuff it full of old paper, come back, and check into the hotel—somewhere on the seventh floor, if possible. I want you to wait right here. Promise me you won't go out until I get back."

"I promise."

"And don't answer the phone," Mason warned.

"I . . . all right, if you say so."

"I say so," Mason told her.

The lawyer walked to the door, turned, smiled, and said, "You'll be all right, Diana."

Her eyes started to blink rapidly. "You're wonderful," she said. "I wish I'd told you all about it when I first came to your office."

"You can say that again," Mason told her. "We might have headed off that damned auditor. As it is now, you're hooked."

"What do you mean?"

"Figure it out," Mason said. "We're starting a little late. You've come to Los Angeles, registered in a hotel under an assumed name. You have a bag containing five thousand dollars in currency. And if the company where you work *should* happen to be short five thousand dollars, and if your brother *should* happen to die, and if you're arrested before you get that cashier's check—figure where you'll be."

Mason walked out as her mouth slowly opened. He closed the door gently behind him.

Chapter Six

THE LAWYER took the elevator to the lobby, went to a baggage store two doors down the street, selected a suitcase, paid for it; then he crossed to a secondhand bookstore.

"I'm looking for some books dealing with the history of early California and, particularly, with the discovery of gold," he said.

The clerk led him to a shelf.

"Do you," Mason asked, "have paperback books?"

"Oh, yes, we have quite a selection."

"I also want to get some of those books for lighter reading," Mason said. "I'll pick out some."

Ten minutes later Mason presented himself at the checking-out desk with an armful of books.

The cashier scanned the penciled prices marked on the title pages, gave Mason the total figure, $27.85.

"All right," Mason said, "I'll . . . why not put them in this suitcase?"

The clerk, his attention drawn to the suitcase, leaned

forward to pick it up and make sure it was empty, then smiled and said, "That's quite all right. Put them in there if you want."

Mason put the books in the suitcase, paid the bill, walked back to the Hotel Willatson, said, "I'm going to be here probably overnight. I'd like to have a room somewhere above the fifth floor. I don't like traffic noises."

"I can let you have eleven-eighty-four," the room clerk said, "if you're only going to be here one night, Mister . . . uh . . ."

"Mason," Perry Mason said. "I prefer to be a little lower than the eleventh floor. What have you got on the eighth?"

"We're all taken up."

"The seventh?"

"I have one room on the seventh floor—seven-eighty-nine. It's a slightly larger room than our average and a little more expensive. . . ."

"That's all right," Mason said, "I'll take it. I'm likely to be here only one night."

The lawyer registered, gave a bellboy a dollar to take his bag and escort him up to the room, waited until the bellboy had withdrawn; then put the room key in his pocket and walked down the hall to 767.

He tapped gently on the panels.

Diana Douglas opened the door.

"Mr. Mason," she said, "I've been thinking over what you said. It's—I'm afraid I'm in a terrible position."

"It'll be all right," Mason told her, "I'll take charge."

"You're going to—to need more than the money I gave you."

"Unfortunately," Mason said, "I spent a large amount of the money you gave me trying to check up on you and get back of the falsehoods you had told me. As it is now . . ."

The lawyer broke off as a knuckle tapped gently on the door.

Diana Douglas raised inquiring eyebrows.

Mason strode across the room, opened the door to confront an alert-looking young woman with blonde hair, blue eyes, and that something in her bearing which radiated competency and ability to look after herself under any circumstances.

The woman smiled at him and said, "I recognize you, Mr. Mason, but you probably don't know me. I'm from—well, I'm Stella Grimes."

"Come in, Stella," Mason said.

The lawyer closed the door and said, "Stella, this is Diana Douglas. She's registered here as Diana Deering. You're going to take over."

"Who am I?" Stella asked. "Diana Douglas or Diana Deering? . . . And how do you do, Diana. I'm pleased to meet you."

"As far as the hotel is concerned you're Diana Deering," Mason said. "I'll let you read an ad which appeared in the paper."

Mason handed her a copy of the ad which Diana had inserted in the paper and which was signed "36-24-36."

"I see, Mr. Mason," Stella said, reading the ad carefully. Then she looked at Diana, looked at Perry Mason, and said, "Precisely what do I do?"

"You identify yourself here as Diana Deering," Mason said. "You sit tight and await developments and you report."

"Report on what?"

"On everything."

"Can you give me any line on what is supposed to happen?" she asked. "I take it that I'm supposed to be here to make a cash payment. Suppose someone turns up and wants that cash?"

"Then you stall," Mason said.

She nodded, took a card from her purse, scribbled something on it, and said, "You'll probably want one of my cards, Mr. Mason."

The lawyer took the card she had given him. On the back was scribbled, *"I've seen her before. I was the operative in the taxicab with Paul Drake last night."*

Mason slipped the card in his pocket. "Exactly," he said, "I'll call you by name if I have to, but in the meantime I want you to impress upon the clerk that if someone calls and asks for you by the code numbers of thirty-six, twenty-four, thirty-six that the call is to be put through. You think you can make up a good story?"

"I can try," she said.

"What do you have in the way of baggage?" Mason asked.

"Just this purse that I brought in with me. I was instructed not to attract attention by coming in with any more than this."

"You can buy what you need at the department stores and have it sent in," Mason said.

"Any idea how long I'll be here?"

"It may be only a day. It may be three or four days. Just sit down and make yourself at home. I'll be right back."

"I'll take your suitcase down to Room Seven-eighty-nine, Diana," he said. "Later on I'll check out with it and give it to you in San Francisco. In the meantime, you take this key, go on down to seven-eighty-nine, and wait. Take that black bag and your purse with you. I'll be seeing you in seven-eighty-nine in a few minutes. You use that room until you're ready to get the cashier's check and leave for the airport. Don't come back to this room under any circumstances and don't try to leave Room Seven-eighty-nine until I give you the all-clear sign."

"Any idea when that will be?" she asked.

"When I think the coast is clear."

"Suppose the banks close before you say it's okay for me to leave?"

"Then you'll have to keep the money with you until you get to San Francisco. Get the cashier's check there, but don't enter the office tomorrow until you have that check. When the office opens tomorrow I'll be on hand to help. We'll fix up the details before we leave Room Seven-eighty-nine. In the meantime, I want you out of here."

She nodded, said, "I want to get a couple of things from the bathroom."

Stella Grimes said to Mason, "You'd better brief *me*

a little more. What happens if someone calls on me by this number, wants me to meet him with a sum of cash?"

"Stall it along and notify Paul," Mason told her.

"And if there isn't time for that?"

"Make time."

"Am I to have any idea what it's all about?" she asked.

"Nothing that I can tell you," Mason said.

"Am I the party that's being blackmailed?"

"No," Mason said, "you're a girl friend, an angel who's going to put up the money, but before you put up the money you want to be absolutely certain that you're getting what you're paying for. You're a fairly wealthy young woman, but you're rough, you're tough, you're hard-boiled. You know your way around. . . . Got a gun?"

By way of answer she reached down the V of her blouse and suddenly produced a wicked-looking, snub-nosed revolver.

"I'm wearing my working bra," she said as Diana emerged from the bathroom, her hands filled with toilet articles.

"Good enough," Mason told her. "I hope you don't have to reach for it, but I'm glad you've got it. We don't know with whom we're dealing."

"Have there been—other payments?" she asked.

"That we don't know," Mason said. "The present demand is for five grand. The probabilities are there's been one earlier payment and this is—you know, the old story, the guy hates to be a blackmailer. He wants to begin life all over again. He had intended to collect a thousand or so every few months, but he just can't live with himself on that kind of a deal. If he can get five grand he's going to buy a little farm way out in the sticks and forget all about his past and turn over a new leaf.

"In that case he'll tell the sucker he'll be done with payments forevermore, and all that sort of talk. . . . You know the line."

"I know the line," she said, smiling. "I've heard it."

Mason took Diana's suitcase and said, "We're taking this down to seven-eighty-nine, Diana. You take that black bag. Be sure to follow instructions."

"And I'll see you in San Francisco?"

"That's right. I'll get in touch with you. Put your phone number and address here in my notebook. But stay in seven-eighty-nine until I give you an all-clear."

The lawyer handed her his open notebook. Diana took it and carefully made the notations Mason asked, picked up the black bag, gave Stella her hand, said, "Thanks, sister. Be careful, and keep wearing that bra."

She turned to Perry Mason and said, "You're all right. You're good. . . . Let me carry my suitcase. I'll wait. I have the key to seven-eighty-nine." Impulsively she kissed him on the cheek, picked up the suitcase, the black bag and purse, crossed swiftly to the door, opened it, and was gone.

Mason settled himself in a chair, motioned for Stella to be seated, said, "I'm playing this pretty much in the dark myself, Stella. The blackmailer will be expecting the pay-off will be made by a man. You'll have to act the part of the financial angel, probably related to the sucker. However, you're skeptical, hard-boiled, and—"

The lawyer broke off as knuckles tapped on the door.

"This may be it," he said. "Gosh, I hope Diana got down to seven-eighty-nine and out of sight."

The knuckles sounded again.

The lawyer went to the door, opened it, and said, "Yes, what is it?"

The man who stood on the threshold was a small man in his early thirties. He had black hair which was very sleek and glossy, parted in the middle and curled back from his forehead at the temples. He was wearing dark glasses and well-pressed brown slacks with a darker brown sport coat. His shirt was tan, and an expensive bolo tie furnished ornamentation.

"How do you do?" he said. "I called in response to an ad in the paper. I . . ." He broke off as he caught sight of Stella Grimes.

"That's all right," Mason said. "Come in."

The man hesitated, then extended a well-manicured hand, the nails highly polished, the skin soft and elaborately cared for.

"Cassel," he said, smiling, "C - A - S - S - E - L. I had hardly expected you would come down in person, Mr.—"

Mason held up his left hand as he shook Cassel's right hand.

"No names, please."

"All right, no names," Cassel said.

He regarded Stella Grimes appraisingly, as a cattle buyer might size up a prime heifer. There was a puzzled frown on his forehead which speedily gave way to an oily smile.

"We'll dispense with introductions," Mason said abruptly.

Cassel said, "As you wish. However, we don't put on our best performances in front of an audience, you know." He made a deprecatory gesture. "I confess *I* get stage fright," he said. "I may not be able to recall my lines at all."

Stella said, "Perhaps you two would like to have me go in the bathroom and close the door."

"No, no, no," Cassel said. "Nowhere in the room, please. I am *very* self-conscious."

Mason laughed. "Mr. Cassel and I have some very private business to discuss, Stella. I'm sorry that you and I didn't have more of an opportunity to talk, but it follows that we'll get together sometime later. I dislike these interruptions as much as you do, but that's the way things go. . . . Mr. Cassel and I are going to have a business talk, and *following* that I'll be in and out for a while, but I'll give you a ring whenever I'm at liberty. However, don't wait for my call. Just *follow* your own inclinations."

Stella Grimes regarded Mason thoughtfully for a few seconds, then said, "I think I've got it," to Mason, and, turning to Cassel said, "Good-by, Mr. Cassel."

She walked casually over to Perry Mason, put her lips up to be kissed as in a pleasant but often-repeated salutation of affection, then left the room.

"Nice babe," Cassel said, eying Mason.

Mason shrugged. "I like her."

"Known her long?"

Mason smiled. "Not long enough."

"You're not handing me *that* line," Cassel said.

"I'm handing you nothing."

"You can say that again."

There was a brief period of silence.

"Okay," Cassel said, "let's quit stalling around and get down to business. You brought it with you?"

"Brought what?" Mason asked.

"Now, let's not be cagey about this," Cassel said irritably. "I don't think that you'd be guilty of a breach of faith by trying to blow the whistle but . . . to hell with this stuff, let's take a look."

Cassel strode to the bathroom, jerked the door open, looked around inside, surveyed the walls of the room, moved a couple of pictures looking for a concealed microphone.

"Don't be simple," Mason said when he had finished.

Cassel's eyes were suspicious. "I don't like the way you're going about this," he said.

"What's wrong with the way I'm going about it?"

"You want me to make statements," Cassel said. "I'm not making statements. I'm here. You're here. It's your move."

Mason said, "I'm the one that should be suspicious. What made you so long showing up?"

"I had other matters which took me out of town for a while," Cassel said. "I called as soon as I came back and got free. . . . By the way, there was an ad in one of the evening papers. Do you know anything about that?"

Mason said, "I know enough about it to know that I wasted a lot of time giving the occupants of a taxicab an opportunity to give me the double take."

"And you received no signal?"

"No."

Cassel shook his head. "I don't like that. I don't like that at all. It means some third party is trying to chisel in on the deal."

"*You* don't like it," Mason said. "How do you suppose I feel about it? What the hell are you trying to do?"

Cassel thought for a moment, glanced at Mason, looked away, looked back at Mason again, frowned, said, "There's something familiar about your face. Have I ever met you before?"

"I don't think so."

"Well, every once in a while you —What a minute, wait a minute . . . I've seen your picture somewhere!"

"That's not at all impossible," Mason conceded.

"Hell's bells," Cassel said, "I've got it. Why dammit, you're a lawyer. Your name is Mason."

Mason didn't let his face change expression by so much as the flicker of an eyelash.

"That's right," he said, "Perry Mason."

"What are you trying to pull?" Cassel asked. "That wasn't part of the deal. I don't want to have any business dealings with any damn lawyer."

Mason smiled affably. "I'm not any damn lawyer," he said. "I'm a particularly special, high-priced lawyer."

"I'll say you are," Cassel said, edging toward the door. "What the hell's the matter with you, Mason? Are you crazy? You act as though you've got the room bugged.

You know as well as I do that if you're trying to blow any whistles you're cutting your client's throat. You're acting just as if this was some kind of a shakedown."

Mason said nothing.

"You know the proposition," Cassel said. "It's a business proposition. Your client doesn't have any choice in the matter but, under the circumstances, he can't have any protection. Any agreement that's made isn't worth the powder and shot to blow it up."

Mason said, "That doesn't prevent me from representing my client."

Cassel sneered. "It means that we've had our sights too low," he said. "If your client has got money enough to pay a high-priced lawyer a fat fee in a deal of this kind we've been too naïve. I don't blame you, I blame us. We aren't asking enough."

"Keep talking," Mason said. "I'm listening."

Cassel, annoyed now, said, "This isn't a payoff. This is something your client owes. . . . I'm not going to argue with you, Mason, have you got it or haven't you?"

"If you're referring to the money," Mason said, "I don't have it, and if I did have it I wouldn't pay it over on the strength of any proposition you've made so far."

"What's wrong with my proposition?" Cassel asked.

"You said it yourself. Any agreement is worthless. You could come back tomorrow and begin all over again."

"I wouldn't be foolish enough to do that," Cassel said.

"Why not?"

"Well, it wouldn't be . . . ethical."

Mason laughed.

Cassel's face darkened. "Look, Mason, you're supposed to be high-powered. You're supposed to be the last word. But all you're doing so far is making it tough for your client. He had a chance to get off the hook at a bargain price. Now, things are going up."

"Don't say that," Mason said, "or prices may go down."

"You think you can pull a rabbit out of a hat?" Cassel asked sneeringly.

Mason said, "That's what I'm noted for, pulling rabbits out of hats and coming up with another ace when it's least expected."

Cassel started angrily for the door, turned, said, "Look, Mason, let's be businesslike. Your client pays five grand and that's all there is to it."

"And what does he get in return for the five grand?"

"Immunity."

"What about the proofs?"

Cassel's face showed surprise. "What are you talking about, the proofs?"

Mason recovered easily. "The proofs of your integrity, of the fact that my client has immunity."

"Draw up an agreement," Cassel said.

"You said yourself it wouldn't be worth anything."

"Not in court," Cassel said, "and not if the right party brings the action. But it closes a lot of doors—all the doors your client needs to worry about."

"I'll think it over," Mason conceded.

"Think it over, hell! You haven't got a lot of time to think things over. This is a hot deal. If you're going to go for it, you've got to move and move fast."

"Where can I reach you?" Mason asked.

Cassel surveyed him thoughtfully. "You're asking a lot of questions."

"All right," Mason said, "where can I leave the money—if I decide to leave the money?"

Cassel said, "Look, your phone number is listed. You have an office. I don't know what you're doing here in the hotel. I'll give you a call from a pay station at your office."

"When?"

"When I get damned good and ready," Cassel said. He opened the door and walked out, slamming the door behind him.

Mason went to the telephone, put a call through the switchboard to Paul Drake's office.

"Perry Mason talking, Paul. Did Stella Grimes phone in for an operative to do a tailing job?"

"Haven't heard from her," Drake said. "The last I knew she was in the Willatson Hotel. Weren't you with her?"

"I was," Mason said. "I had a man I wanted followed. I tried to give her a signal."

"If you gave her a signal, she got it all right," Drake said. "She's a bright babe. Was there any reason why she couldn't do the tailing job herself?"

"The only trouble is, the subject knows her," Mason said. "A stranger would have been better."

"Well, she probably didn't have time to phone in. What was it, a rush job?"

"It was one hell of a rush job."

"You'll be hearing from her," Drake predicted.

Mason hung up the phone, walked casually around the room, again picked up the telephone, said to the hotel operator, "Ring Room Seven-eighty-nine, please."

It was some time before Diana Douglas answered the phone.

"Yes?" she asked.

Mason said, "It took you a while to answer, Diana."

"I didn't know whether I should answer or not. How's everything down your way? I thought you were coming to—"

"We were interrupted," Mason said. "The other party to the transaction showed up."

"You mean . . . you mean the blackmailer?"

"Yes."

"What happened?"

"We stalled around for a while," Mason said, "and, unfortunately, he made me."

"What do you mean by that?"

"He knew who I was. He recognized me from the photographs he had seen in the papers from time to time."

"Is that bad?" she asked.

"It may be good," Mason said. "I think he was just a little frightened. . . . I just wanted to tell you to sit tight until you hear from me. It's *very* important that you keep under cover."

"I should be—well, shouldn't I be getting my ticket back to San Francisco? And the banks will be closed here."

"We can't hurry this now," Mason said. "There may be developments. Wait a few minutes—or up to an hour—until I have a chance to join you. Don't try to leave that room until I give you a signal that everything's in the clear."

Chapter Seven

MASON STRETCHED out in Room 767 at the Willatson Hotel. Despite himself he couldn't refrain from glancing at his wristwatch every few minutes. Twice he got up and paced the floor.

The phone rang.

Mason snatched up the instrument. "Yes?" he said.

Diana Douglas' voice said, "Mr. Mason, I'm frightened. Can I come down there and wait where I can be with you?"

"Definitely not," Mason said. "Sit where you are. I'll have instructions for you soon."

"What do you mean by soon?"

"I hope within a few minutes."

"I'm getting the heebie jeebies sitting here all by myself, Mr. Mason, just looking at the walls and . . . well, I feel that we aren't accomplishing anything this way."

"We're accomplishing a lot more than you realize," Mason said, "and it's imperative that you follow instructions. Just sit tight."

The lawyer hung up the telephone, walked over to the window, looked down at the street, came back to his chair, settled himself; then abruptly got up and started pacing the floor.

The doorknob suddenly turned. The door opened and Stella Grimes walked into the room.

"Any luck?" Mason asked.

"Lots of it," she said, tossing a cardboard box on the bed.

Mason raised his eyebrows.

"Clothes," she said. "I picked up a few necessities at the department store because I felt I might have to ride herd on this room. I just snatched up some things and had them wrapped up because I didn't want to keep you waiting."

"What happened?"

"Well," she said, "I got your signal all right. You wanted him followed."

"That's right."

"Well, of course, he knew me by sight. That complicated the job. I felt that the chances that he was living here in the hotel were rather slim. So I went down to the curb, hired a taxicab, and told the driver to just sit there until I told him I wanted to take off.

"Well, it was absurdly simple, so simple in fact that I feel that perhaps it may have been a frame."

"What happened?"

"Our man had his own car, a Cadillac. He had given the doorman a substantial tip to park it for a few minutes in the loading zone. It must have been a pretty good-sized tip because when he came out the doorman was all attention. He ran over and held the car door open for Cassel and bowed his thanks as Cassel drove off."

"You followed?"

"That's right."

"Get the license number?"

She took a notebook from her pocket and read off the license number, "WVM five-seven-four."

"Could you tail him?" Mason asked.

"It was easy. He went to the Tallmeyer Apartments. Drove right into the garage in the basement of the apartment house and didn't come out."

"So what did you do?" Mason asked.

"I had my taxi driver drive three blocks to where a car was pulling out from the curb. I said, 'Follow that car but don't let him know he's being followed.' "

"Good work," Mason said.

"Well, of course, this driver got mixed up in traffic. We lost out on a traffic signal and I shrugged my shoulders and said, 'Well, that's the best we can do.' Paid off the cab and took another one and came back here to the hotel. I didn't want the cab driver giving me a double cross and tipping Cassel off, and, as it is, he thinks I'm some sort of a nut. At least, I hope he does."

Mason picked up the phone, said to the operator, "Give me an outside line," then gave the number of the Drake Detective Agency.

"Paul in?" he asked the switchboard operator.

"He just came in, Mr. Mason," she said, recognizing his voice.

"Put him on, will you please?"

Drake's voice came on the line, "Hello."

"Perry Mason, Paul."

"Where are you?"

"At the Willatson Hotel with Stella Grimes. She's back now."

"Doing any good?"

"I think we've struck pay dirt. I want to find out the owner of a Cadillac automobile, license number WVM five-seven-four, and if the owner lives at the Tallmeyer Apartments I'd like to try to find out a little bit about him without doing anything that would arouse suspicion."

Drake said, "Della was asking if it's all right to call you."

"She'd best not," Mason said. "I'll call the office from time to time and see if there's anything important. Was there something in particular on her mind?"

"I don't think so, except that you had a few appointments she had to get you out of with a story about you being called out of town on important business."

"I think that's just what's going to happen," Mason said.

"On the square?"

"On the square. . . . How long will it take you to find out about that car registration?"

"I can have that right quick."

"I'll call back," Mason said. "Get on it as fast as you can."

"How's Stella doing?" Drake asked.

"Fine," Mason said.

"Okay, if you want anything, just put in a call. It'll cost you money, but you'll get the service."

"Will do," Mason said, and hung up.

"Gosh, that guy was mad," Stella said. "You really must have pinned his ears back!"

Mason grinned. "How did you know he was mad, Stella?"

"The way he walked, the way he looked, and the way he left himself wide open."

"I guess he was disappointed," Mason said. "He was expecting a soft touch."

"I'll bet he thought he'd run full speed into a brick wall instead," she observed. "He certainly was one very mad citizen."

The lawyer looked at his wristwatch. "Hold the fort a minute, Stella," he said. "I'm going down the hall. If anything should happen that would complicate the situation hang the DO NOT DISTURB sign on the outside of the door. If Paul Drake phones while I'm down there tell him to call me in that room."

Mason walked down to Room 789 and tapped on the door.

Diana Douglas threw the door open.

"Don't do that!" Mason said.

"Do what?"

"Be so eager," Mason said. "Don't open that door until you find out who it is."

"I'm all on edge," she said. "I sit here and thoughts are running through my head. I just can't take this waiting game, Mr. Mason."

Mason said, "Listen very carefully, Diana. How much money do you have?"

"I told you, five thousand dollars."

"That isn't what I meant. I want to know how much you have outside of that."

"I drew out six hundred dollars from my savings account when I left. I wanted to have enough to give you a retainer and—"

"The money that you gave me didn't come out of the five thousand dollars then?"

"No."

"You don't have any idea on earth what this is all about? I want you to be frank, now."

She lowered her eyes. "Well, I suppose it's some kind of an indiscretion that Edgar—well, something he got himself mixed up with. . . . Oh, you know how those rackets go, some kind of a badger game or photographs or— Why do you ask me these questions, Mr. Mason?"

"Because," Mason said, "I think we may be following a wrong trail, barking up a wrong tree. Tell me as much as you can about Edgar, only condense it."

"Well," she said, motioning for him to sit down, and seating herself on the edge of the bed, "Edgar is naïve. He's—I won't say he's weak, but he is easily influenced, and I suppose I haven't been of too much help to him trying to make things a little easier for him. I guess life wasn't meant to be that way, Mr. Mason. I guess a man has to develop himself by having things made a little difficult at times instead of having someone whom he looks up to who can smooth things out and take some of the load off his shoulders."

"That's what I was coming to," Mason said. "Do you think there's anything in Edgar's past that would have caused him to come to you with a sum of money and ask you to bail him out?"

"I just don't know, Mr. Mason."

"He could have been coming to you?"

"He could have been, but everything indicates he was going to come here to Los Angeles and try to deal with this thirty-six-twenty-four-thirty-six situation."

"And you have no clue as to what that situation is?"

"No."

"Your brother gambled from time to time?" Mason asked.

She chose her words carefully. "Edgar was impulsive."

"He gambled from time to time?"

"Don't all men?"

"He gambled from time to time?"

"Yes," she flared. "You don't need to cross-examine me like that. He gambled from time to time."

"Where?"

"Where do men usually gamble? Sometimes he put two dollars on a horse. Sometimes he put ten dollars on a horse."

"Las Vegas—Reno?"

"He would go to Las Vegas once in a while."

"How much did he ever win?"

"I don't know. I don't think he won much."

"What was the most he ever lost?"

"Eight hundred dollars."

"How do you know?"

"He told me."

"Why did he tell you?"

"Because I'm his sister."

"Why did he tell you?"

"I told you," she blazed back at him. I'm his sister. What are you doing, trying to break down my story?"

"Why did he tell you?" Mason asked.

"All right," she said, lowering her voice, "I had to bail him out. He only had two hundred and I had to make good to the extent of six hundred dollars. He had given a check in Las Vegas and—well, you know how they are."

"How are they?" Mason asked.

She shrugged her shoulders. "I don't know, but the story is that if you gamble on credit with professional gamblers you have to make good or else."

"And Edgar was frightened?"

"Terribly frightened."

"In other words," Mason said, "I'm trying to establish a pattern. When Edgar gets into real trouble, he comes to you. You've been something of a sister and a mother to him."

"Well," she said thoughtfully, "I guess that's right."

"So, if Edgar was in some trouble where he had to raise five thousand dollars, the assumption is he would have told you."

"Unless he—well, it might have been something that he wouldn't have wanted to talk to me about. You know, men can get into scrapes of that sort where they wouldn't want their family to know just what had happened."

"Who told you that?" Mason asked.

"Why, I . . . I've read it."

"Ever talk with Edgar about anything like that?"

"No."

"Know anything about Edgar's sex life?"

"Virtually nothing."

Mason regarded her thoughtfully. He said, "There's a United Airlines plane leaving here for San Francisco at six twenty-seven. I want you to be on that plane.

"I'm going to escort you to the elevator. When you get to the lobby, walk across the lobby casually. Don't look around as though you might be afraid someone was trying to follow you. We'll walk two blocks down the street. There's a taxi stand down there. I'll put you in a cab. Go to the Union Station. When you get to the Union Station, try to make sure that you're not being followed. Then go out, get a cab, and go to the airport. When you get to the airport, wait."

"For what?"

"I'll try to meet you just before you get on the plane. I'll have your baggage. I'll check out of the hotel within an hour or so. That'll give me time to get to my apartment and pack a bag. I'll take my bags and your suitcase and join you at the airport."

"But what about this bag that has the—you know, the money in it?"

"The banks are closed now," Mason said. "You've got to take a chance with that because I want you to be sure and have a cashier's check made to you as trustee when you walk into the office in the morning.

"The minute the banks open in San Francisco, get that cashier's check. Then go to the office just as if nothing out of the ordinary had ever happened. I'll meet you there when you come in. That should be about ten-thirty. Let's have that as the deadline. Don't arrive before ten-thirty. Don't be any later than that if you can avoid it."

The telephone rang.

Mason said, "I think that's for me."

He picked up the instrument, said a cautious, "Hello."

Drake's voice, cheerfully routine, came over the line, "Hi, Perry. Got most of the information you want. It was like rolling off a log."

"What is it?"

"The Cadillac you wanted is registered under the name of Moray Cassel, nine-o-six Tallmeyer Apartments. I've got that much. I haven't been able to find out much about Cassel's habits as yet, but he's been a resident there for something over a year."

"Well, I'll be damned," Mason said in an undertone.

"Something wrong?"

"The guy gave me his right name," Mason said. "You could certainly have fooled me. I had him sized up as a blackmailing pimp, a damned good, prosperous, shrewd pimp."

"And he isn't?" Drake asked.

"That I'll have to find out," Mason said.

"You want him tailed?"

"No. The guy is either too dumb to be true or too smart to be trapped, and I want to find out which it is before I get my feet wet."

"Okay, let me know if there's anything else you want."

"Will do," Mason said, and hung up.

Diana, watching Mason with anxious eyes, said, "Is something wrong?"

Mason, frowning thoughtfully, let the question go unanswered for a few seconds, then said, "I don't know. I seem to have made a mistake in sizing up a situation."

"In what way?"

Mason said, "Thanks to good detective work on the part of the Drake Detective Agency, we have run the blackmailer to ground. His name is Moray Cassel. He drives a Cadillac automobile. He lives in the Tallmeyer Apartments, apartment nine-o-six. But when he came to call on us he gave us his real name. He had his Cadillac parked right in front of the door, having given the doorman a good tip to see that it was left where it would be readily accessible in the parking space reserved for incoming guests with baggage."

"Well, what's wrong about that?" Diana asked. "A lot of people who are on brief errands give the doorman a good tip to keep an eye on their cars. That's the way the doormen make a living. They—"

Mason shook his head. "It isn't that, Diana," he interrupted. "The man simply wasn't that kind of a citizen."

"How do you know?"

Mason said, "Well, I have to admit that this is a time when I may have led with my chin, but I sized the man up as a pimp."

"How, for heaven's sake?"

"His appearance. His manner. Everything about him."

"Mr. Mason, do you mean to tell me you can just take a look at a man like that, have a quick conversation with him, and know that he's . . . well, what you call a pimp?"

"No," Mason said at length, "I won't go that far, Diana. And remember when I say the guy's a pimp, I don't mean that he's actually engaged in pimping, I mean he's that type of citizen. He's one who would make his living out of representing a woman in a blackmail scheme."

"But how in the world can you possibly tell? What is there about a man of that sort, the way he dresses, that . . . I just don't get it."

"It's not any one particular thing," Mason said. "It's a combination of things. You take a man who's making his living directly or indirectly out of women, and he knows there's something wrong inside. He tries to cover it up. He tries to square himself with himself. He tries to put the best possible veneer on top of what's underneath in order to hide the rotten part.

"So he goes in for a faultless personal appearance. His shoes are always shined. His trousers are sharply creased. He wears expensive shirts and ties. His nails are always well manicured. The skin of his hands is well cared for. His hair is cut, combed, and brushed so that it makes a flattering appearance in the mirror.

"Then there's his voice. There's something about it. A voice that isn't used to carrying weight with the world in general but is sharply authoritative in dealing with a situation which he thinks he can handle. It lacks tone and timbre. You have the feeling that if he became enraged and flew off the handle his voice would rise to a sharp falsetto."

"And this man, Cassel, had those points?"

"He had those points," Mason said.

"What did he want?"

"He wanted money."

"Did he say how much?"

"He wanted the bundle, five grand."

"And what did you tell him?"

"I stalled him along."

"Did he go for it?"

"He didn't like it."

"Did he feel that you were—?"

"As I told you, he recognized me," Mason said. "I've had my picture in the newspapers too often. He knew that he was dealing with Perry Mason, an attorney, and he didn't like any part of it."

"And you never did find out what he wanted, what he had on my brother, Edgar?"

Mason shook his head. "It evidently isn't the ordinary kind of blackmail deal," he said.

"You think it was something . . . well, worse than what you call the ordinary blackmail?"

"It could have been," Mason said. "He acted as though he really had the winning hand."

"What's he going to do next?"

Mason shrugged his shoulders, said, "That's something we'll have to wait for."

"Mr. Mason, suppose it could be something—well, *real* serious?"

"You don't make a pass at a guy for five thousand bucks on squaring a ticket for parking in front of a fire hydrant," Mason said. "Whatever it is, it's something serious."

"Look, Mr. Mason, I've . . . I could raise money if . . ."

Mason said, "Forget it. It's against my policy to pay off blackmailers. To hell with them. Come on, Diana, we're going to leave here casually. We won't be carrying anything except your purse and that black bag with the money in it. I'm going to walk with you through the lobby and out the front door. As we cross the lobby, be talking and laughing. You know, the quick, nervous laugh of a woman who realizes that she's embarking on an adventure which may have romantic overtones. I don't want anyone to think that you may be surreptitiously leaving the hotel.

"Now, after we've walked across the lobby, we're going down the street a couple of blocks to a taxicab stand. You remember and follow instructions. Get in a taxicab and pull away from the curb. Go to the Union Depot. Mingle around with the crowds. Switch cabs. Go to the airport and get that plane for San Francisco. . . . Hold everything. I'll see if I can get reservations."

Mason picked up the phone and asked for an outside line. He gave the number of United Airlines, got the reservations desk, and asked for two tickets to San Francisco on the flight leaving at six twenty-seven.

The lawyer nodded his satisfaction, said, "We'll

pick up the tickets at the airport. Put them both under the name of Perry Mason. . . . That's right,
Perry Mason, the lawyer. I'm listed in the phone books.
I have an Air Travel Card and— That's fine! I'll pick
up one ticket myself. Give the other one to a Miss Diana Douglas. Hold them right up until plane time, if
you will.

"Thank you very much!"

Mason hung up the telephone, said, "Everything's
all set, Diana. Ask for a ticket that's held in the name of
Perry Mason. I'll see you aboard the plane. I'll have
your suitcase with me when I check out of the hotel
here. Now, remember that if anything happens to that
bag of money you're carrying, you're stuck. You're behind the eight ball. You're in trouble."

"I know," she said. "I've been carrying it with me
and I . . . I can hardly sleep worrying about it. I
know that if anything happens to it I'm never going to
be able to work things out. But I've got by so far and,
after all, Mr. Mason, who knows I'm carrying five thousand dollars?"

"Too many people by this time," Mason said grimly.
"Come on, Diana, put on your best smile and we're going to go down to the lobby, out the front door, and
down to the taxicab stand. You're going to be laughing
and talking and I'll try a wisecrack now and then. . . .
Come on, let's go. I've got an idea this hotel may be a
darn poor place for you from now on. . . . You'll have
some time to wait at the airport, but try to be as incon-
spicuous as possible and get aboard the plane just as
soon as the doors are open for boarding."

Chapter Eight

MASON RETURNED to Room 767 at the hotel, knocked at the door, and when Stella admitted him said, "Well, I got rid of the bait in the case. She'll join me at the airport. Let's hope nothing happens until we get off."

"You think she's in danger?"

"Not danger exactly, but this guy Cassel worries me. He may be smarter than I had him pegged. I've had an uneasy feeling about Diana ever since I arrived here at the hotel. She left too wide a back trail and—"

The lawyer paused as the sharp rap of knuckles sounded on the door. He turned back and said to Stella Grimes in a low voice, "Those are masculine knuckles and they sound imperative."

"Cassel coming back?" she asked.

Mason shook his head. "He's a soft, sneaky knocker. These are the knuckles of authority—either the house detective, or—"

He was interrupted by another knock and a voice said, "Open up, please. This is the police."

Mason said to Stella Grimes, "Let me do as much of the talking as possible."

Mason opened the door.

Two plain-clothes men, standing in the hallway, showed surprise as they recognized the lawyer.

"Perry Mason," one said, "what are *you* doing *here?*"

"The question," Mason said, "is what *you* are doing here."

"We prefer to discuss it inside rather than in the corridor," the spokesman said, and pushed his way into the room, holding in his hand a leather folder displaying a badge. "Los Angeles police," he said.

"And what brings you here?" Mason asked.

The officers ignored him temporarily, looked at Stella Grimes. One of the officers nodded at the other. "Age twenty-two, five-feet-two, a hundred and sixteen pounds, blonde, blue eyes, good figure," he said.

The other nodded.

The two officers helped themselves to chairs, and one said, "We want to ask a few questions."

"Very well," Mason said, "go ahead."

"Is your name Diana Douglas?" one of the officers asked Stella Grimes.

"Now, just a minute," Mason said. "Let's do this thing in an orderly manner. Why do you come here?"

"We don't have to tell you that."

"No, but you have to tell the young woman that. Do you suspect her of a crime?"

"We're acting on telegraphed instructions from the San Francisco police. We're trying to get some information. We want to ask some questions, that's all."

"Do you suspect this young woman of any crime?"

"We don't know. We haven't the faintest idea."

"You're acting for the San Francisco police?"

"Yes."

"Do the San Francisco police suspect her of any crime?"

"We're not mind readers. We don't know."

"Then," Mason said, "since you're acting for and on behalf of the San Francisco police, and since you don't know whether the San Francisco police suspect her of any crime, before she answers *any* questions you had better advise her as to her constitutional rights."

"As if she didn't know them," the officer said.

Mason smiled. "Tell that to the Supreme Court."

"All right, all right," the officer said. "We want you to answer a few questions, Miss. We're not making any specific charges. We're not here to take you into custody, but we do want to ask you some questions.

"You are entitled to remain silent if you wish. You don't have to make any statement. You are entitled to have an attorney represent you at all times. If you don't have money enough to secure an attorney, we will secure one to act on your behalf. However, we want it understood that anything you do say may be used against you. Now then, do you wish an attorney?"

Stella started to say something when Mason motioned her to silence. "She's got one," he said.

"You're representing her?"

"Yes."

"What are you doing here—Miss Douglas, is it?"

"She's here on business," Mason said.

"What sort of business?"

"Personal business."

"Miss Douglas, were you aware that a relatively large sum of cash was being kept in the vault at the Escobar Import and Export Company where you work in San Francisco?"

"No comment," Mason said.

"Now, wait a minute," the officer said. "You're injecting yourself into this thing and you're just making it worse for this young lady. All we're trying to do is to elicit information."

"Why?"

"Because San Francisco wants that information."

"I take it there's a crime involved?"

"We're not sure. San Francisco isn't sure."

"I think, under the circumstances, my client doesn't care to answer any questions until the situation is clarified," Mason said.

"You're forcing us to report to San Francisco that there's every likelihood that your client is guilty of a substantial embezzlement."

"Indeed!" Mason said. "How much of an embezzlement?"

"The audit hasn't been completed," the officer said, "but it's a substantial amount—over twenty thousand dollars."

"How much?" Mason exclaimed, surprise showing in his voice.

"You heard me, over twenty grand."

"That's a lot of money to embezzle from one company," Mason said.

"There *have* been embezzlements involving larger sums," the officer said.

"Then there has been a crime committed in San Francisco?"

"If you're referring to the embezzlement, it looks that way."

"And San Francisco suspects my client of embezzling the money?"

"I haven't said that—yet."

"But you want to ask questions about it?"

"Listen, Mason, you're making things rather difficult and you're getting mighty hard to get along with. All we want to do is to ask your client some questions about how the cash is kept in that company, about who has the authority to draw out cash, and, generally, things about the bookkeeping end of it. For your information, that company seems to keep perfectly huge sums of liquid cash available, and we'd like to know why.

"We'd also like to know how many people have the combination to the vault and how it is possible for a company to run up a shortage of that sort without somebody checking it earlier."

"It's been going on for a long time?" Mason asked.

"We don't know," the officer said. "That's what we're trying to find out. We're simply trying to get information."

"But you think my client *may* have embezzled that money?" Mason asked.

"Not exactly," the officer said. "I'll put it this way. We won't say that we've uncovered any evidence which makes it appear that it's a physical impossibility for her to have been guilty of embezzlement, but, on the other hand, we haven't uncovered any evidence which points to her—as yet."

"Except in a circumstantial way," the other officer said.

"Well, yes," the spokesman conceded.

Mason smiled and said, "That makes it very plain, gentlemen. My client is entitled to the advice of counsel."

"That's right. We told her that. There's no question about that."

"And, as her counsel," Mason said, "I advise her to say absolutely nothing."

"You won't even let her talk about the methods of bookkeeping, about the business background of the company?"

"Not a word," Mason said. "Not even to admit her identity."

The two officers looked at each other in frustration and disgust.

"That may not be a very smart thing to do," the spokesman said to Mason.

"Perhaps so," Mason conceded. "I'm not infallible. I make mistakes every so often. . . . How did San Francisco know enough about the situation to send you two hot-footing to the hotel here?"

The officer grinned. "On the advice of counsel, I decline to answer, Mr. Mason."

The lawyer was grave. "You're absolutely entitled to adopt that position. It's a constitutional privilege. You don't need to say a word."

The officers got up, looked belligerently at Stella Grimes.

The spokesman said, "Okay, sister, it's up to you, but let me tell you, you're not being very smart. When we walked in we just wanted information."

"What do you want now?" Mason asked.

"At least twenty grand," the officer said, and then made a parting shot at the lawyer. "Remember it won't do *you* any good to collect a fee out of embezzled money. It can be traced and impounded. . . . I guess that's all."

"See you later," Mason said.

"In court," the officer promised, and walked out.

Mason motioned for silence, said to Stella Grimes in a low voice, "Be careful what you say. They sometimes wait just outside the door."

They were silent for more than a minute; then Mason tiptoed to the door, abruptly jerked it open, and looked up and down the hall.

When he saw there was no one there, the lawyer closed the door and said, "Well, that's a kettle of fish."

"Twenty thousand dollars," Stella Grimes said.

Mason shook his head. "I don't get it," he said, "but I'm on my way to the airport. I'll take the baggage out of my room which has Diana's stuff in it and be on my way. I'm catching that six-twenty-seven flight to San Francisco."

"You're going to see Diana at the airport?"

Mason nodded, said, "She'll join me there. Hold the fort, Stella, and play it by ear. Keep in touch with Paul Drake. . . . Better have your meals sent up to the room for at least twenty-four hours. If you leave the room they may bug it."

She said, "I can get by all right now. What about the switchboard?"

"You'll have to take a chance on that," Mason said. "But don't scatter information around like birdseed. Be cryptic when you call your office, but be sure you get the idea across."

She nodded.

The lawyer left Room 767, walked down to 789, picked up his suitcase and that of Diana Douglas, and called the desk for a boy to assist him.

"Please ask the cashier to have my bill ready," Mason told the desk clerk. "I've received an unexpected long-distance call and I've got to leave at once."

Mason waited until the boy arrived, gave him the bags and a tip, hurried down to the cashier's desk, and explained the situation. "I'm Mr. Mason in Room Seven-eighty-nine. I wanted to stay for a day or two, but I've received a call which makes it imperative that I leave at once. Now, what can we do about the room? I've only been in it a short time. I've used a couple of towels, but the bed hasn't been occupied."

The cashier shook her head. "I'm sorry, Mr. Mason, but we're going to have to charge you for one full day."

Mason made a point of protesting the charge. "But you can put in two new towels and rent the room again."

"I'm sorry, but maid service is cut down at this time of the afternoon and—well, we have a rule, Mr. Mason. I'm sorry."

"All right," the lawyer yielded. "Give me the bill."

He paid in cash, nodded to a bellboy, said, "I want a taxi."

"There's one right outside," the boy said.

Mason gave the boy a good tip, settled himself in the cushions of the taxicab, said in a loud voice, "Take me to the Union Station. Take it easy because I've got a couple of telegrams to read and I want to catch the train to Tucson."

Suddenly Mason, folding the papers which he had taken from his pocket, said, "Hold everything, driver. That telegram really does it."

"You don't want the station?" the driver asked.

"Hell, no," Mason said, "I've simply got to get the plane that leaves for Phoenix and Tucson, so get me to the airport just as fast as you can."

"It's a bad time of day to hit the airport."

"I can't help it, we'll do the best we can."

"When's your plane due out?"

"Five forty-eight," Mason said.

The cab driver threaded his way through traffic, found a through boulevard, and started making time.

Mason sat forward on the edge of the seat, looking at his watch from time to time, occasionally complimenting the cab driver on the time he was making.

The lawyer got to the airport. The cabby honked the horn for a porter.

Mason whipped the door open, said to the porter, "Get those two suitcases on the plane for Tucson."

The lawyer handed the cab driver a ten-dollar bill. "Get going, buddy, before some cop catches up with you. That was a swell ride."

The driver grinned. "This is all for me?"

"Pay the meter and the rest is yours," Mason said.

The driver threw the car into gear.

When he was out of earshot, Mason hurried after the porter.

"I made a mistake," he said, "I was thinking about Tucson. Darn it, I want to get in one of those suitcases. Let me have them." Mason handed the porter a couple of dollars.

"You've got your plane ticket?" the porter asked.

"I've got it," Mason said.

The lawyer went into the waiting room and made a quick survey; then went to the airline counter, picked up one of his tickets, paid for both, checked in Diana's baggage, then walked down to survey the waiting room again. Following this, he strolled casually around, then settled himself comfortably after checking the dummy suitcase in a storage receptacle, and bought a drink.

Five minutes before departure time the lawyer walked in a leisurely manner to the gate and presented his ticket.

"You'll have to hurry," the attendant told him. "The last of the passengers is getting aboard now."

"I'll walk right along," Mason promised.

Mason walked through the door, signaled to the guard, and got aboard the plane just before the portable passageway was pulled back into place.

The hostess at the door looked at him chidingly. "You almost didn't make it," she said.

Mason smiled. "I almost didn't, but it's too hot to hurry."

"There's a seat toward the rear."

"Thank you."

Mason walked the length of the plane, glancing at the faces of the passengers.

After ten or fifteen minutes he walked forward to the lavatory and again took an opportunity to study the faces of the passengers on the plane.

Diana Douglas was not on board.

Mason rode to San Francisco on the plane, took a taxi to a hotel, registered, had dinner, then called the Willatson Hotel, asked for Room 767, and when he heard Stella Grimes' cautious voice on the telephone said, "Recognize the voice, Stella?"

"Yes. Where are you?"

"San Francisco. Did you hear anything from your double?"

"Not a word."

"She was to have taken the same plane I did, but she didn't show up. She didn't leave any message with you?"

"Not a word. I haven't heard a thing."

"Anything from anybody else?"

"Nothing."

Mason said, "I think we've been given a complete runaround on this case, Stella. I'll keep my appointment at ten-thirty tomorrow morning and if nothing happens then we'll wash our hands of the whole business."

"Okay by me. Do I report to you if anything happens?"

"Keep in touch with your employer and I'll contact him. Do you still have your working bra?"

"I have it."

"Keep it," Mason said, "and sleep tight."

Chapter Nine

THE ESCOBAR IMPORT and Export Company had its offices in the United Financial Building.

Mason found from the registry list that the firm had offices on the sixth floor, then retreated to a point near the door where he could watch the people coming in.

The time was 10:20.

At 10:25 Diana Douglas walked through the door.

Mason stepped forward. "Where were you last night?"

She raised tear-swollen eyes; then clutched at his arm as though she needed his physical as well as his mental help.

"Oh, Mr. Mason," she said, "Edgar passed away at three twenty-five this morning."

"I'm so sorry," Mason said, putting his arm around her shoulders. "He meant a lot to you, didn't he?"

"A lot. I was very, very fond of him."

She suddenly buried her head against Mason's shoulder and started to cry.

Mason patted her back. "Now, don't let yourself go, Diana. Remember we have a job to do. You'll have to get your chin up and face the facts."

"I know," she sobbed, "but I . . . I just don't feel that I can take it. . . . If it hadn't been that I'd promised you I'd meet you here I . . . I wanted to telephone Homer Gage and tell him not to expect me. I . . ."

"There, there," Mason said, "we're attracting a lot of attention, Diana. Move over here to the corner and try to get control of yourself. You've got a job to do. You're going to have to go up and face the music."

"How much music?"

"Lots of music."

"What do you mean?"

Mason said, "I'm afraid you're being sucked into a game which is as old as the hills. Someone embezzles a thousand dollars from a company and skips out. Somebody else, who knows what has been going on, calmly reaches in and takes another four thousand out of the till. The man who has absconded with the one thousand dollars gets credit for having embezzled five thousand."

Her eyes, red with crying, widened as she looked at him. "You mean that. . . ?"

"I mean," Mason said, "that the Escobar Import and Export Company is now claiming there's a shortage of twenty thousand dollars."

"*Twenty* thousand dollars!" she repeated, aghast.

"Exactly," Mason said. And then after a moment went on, "How do you come to work? Do you drive or. . . ?"

"No, I take a bus."

"What about arrangements for your brother? Were there any other relatives?"

"No, I got up early this morning and made arrangements."

"Why didn't you take that plane last night as you were instructed?"

"Because I thought someone was following me. Mr. Mason, I felt certain that a man in an automobile followed my taxicab all the way to the Union Depot and then tried to follow me. I tried to lose myself in the crowd, but I don't think I was very successful. I kept having that horrible feeling that this man was spying on me and was where he could see me all the time, so I went into the women's restroom, stayed for a long time, then came out and took a lot of what I suppose you would call evasive tactics. I started through the gate for a train, then doubled back and then, by the time I got to the airport, it was ten minutes too late. The plane had taken off. So then I decided to have dinner and come in on a later plane."

"Why didn't you telephone Paul Drake's office or somebody?"

"I—I never thought of it. I knew you were coming up on that plane and I knew I'd meet you here this morning and—well, I never thought of anything else.

"Then when I got in I telephoned the hospital and found out that my brother was worse and I went up there and—I was with him—when—"

"There, there," Mason said. "You've had a pretty hard row to hoe. Now, what I want you to do is to catch the next bus, go back to your apartment, and try to get some sleep. Do you have any sleeping medicine?"

"Yes, I have some sleeping pills."

"Take them," Mason said. "Go to sleep and forget about everything. . . . Do you have that cashier's check?"

"Yes."

"Give it to me," Mason said. "I probably won't use it, but I'd like to have it. And here's your suitcase."

"What are you going to do?" she asked, giving him the cashier's check.

"I'm going up to the Escobar Import and Export Company and throw a little weight around. At least, I'm going to try to."

"Mr. Mason—twenty thousand dollars. Good Lord!"

"I know," Mason said. "It's a shock."

"But what can we do?"

"That," Mason said, "remains to be seen. The game is old but it's almost infallible. Some poor guy gets to betting on the horses, gets in over his head, takes two or three thousand dollars and skips town, and the smart guy who remains behind cleans out all the cash available and the embezzler is stuck with the whole thing. If they never catch up with him, he's supposed to have taken it all, and if they do catch up with him and he denies that he took anything above two or three thousand, no one believes him. He goes to prison for the whole thing."

Mason put the check in his wallet, then guided her gently toward the street door. "Get on your bus," he said. "Go back to your apartment and go to sleep. Leave

the Escobar Import and Export Company to me. . . .
Do you have a private phone or does it go through the
apartment switchboard?"

"It goes through the apartment switchboard."

"Leave word that you're not to be disturbed," Mason said. "Get some sleep. I have your phone number.
Tell the operator that only calls from me are to be put
through. This is Friday. I'll go back to my office this
afternoon. You can reach me through the Drake Detective Agency if you need me. . . . I'm sorry about
your brother's death. You poor kid, you've had a lot
to put up with during the last few days. Take it easy
and call on me if you need me. . . . Where does your
bus stop?"

"Right here," she said, "at this bus stop. And I owe
you for my plane ticket, Mr. Mason. I remembered you
had ordered two tickets to be charged to you. When I
got to the airport I made a rush for that plane, thinking
it might have been a few minutes late taking off. I was
going to pay for the ticket with my credit card, but I
couldn't find it. I must have lost it, and the girl at the
ticket counter said that the ticket was all paid for,
and—"

"That's all right," Mason said. "Forget it."

He guided her to a wooden bench at the curb. "Take
the first bus home. I'm going up to the office and see
what can be done."

She flung her arms around the lawyer and kissed
him impulsively.

"Mr. Mason, you're *so* wonderful!" she said.

Chapter Ten

Mason stood in the hallway on the sixth floor survey-ing the offices of the Escobar Import and Export Company.

There was a display showing Oriental art goods, carved ivories, and cloisonné.

On the other side of the entrance door the display showed figurines which had a Toltec or Aztec look about them.

Double plate-glass doors opened into a rather shallow showroom in which there were glass shelves containing further specimens of art. The entrance doors had the legend ESCOBAR IMPORT AND EXPORT COMPANY, *Whole-sale Only*.

Mason pushed the doors open and entered the dis-play room. A girl seated at a switchboard smiled me-chanically. "May I help you?" she asked.

Mason said, "I'd like to see Mr. Gage, please."

"Which one? Mr. Franklin Gage or Mr. Homer Gage?"

"Franklin Gage."

"He isn't in. He's out on a business trip."

"Then I'll see Homer Gage."

"What's the name, please?"

"Perry Mason."

"Did you wish to see him about a purchase, Mr. Mason, about some art goods, or. . . ?"

"It's a more personal matter than that," Mason said.

"May I ask what firm you represent?"

"I don't represent any firm," Mason said. "My name is Perry Mason. I'm an attorney from Los Angeles. I happen to be here at the moment to discuss an employee by the name of Diana Douglas."

"Oh, oh!" she said. "Oh, yes . . . yes, indeed. Just a moment!"

She plugged in a line and Mason saw her lips moving rapidly, but the connection of the telephone was so arranged that he couldn't hear her words.

A moment later a door in the back part of the room opened and a heavy-set, chunky individual came striding out, a man in his late thirties, with dark hair which had receded well back from his temples, bushy black eyebrows, keen gray eyes, and tortoise-shell glasses. His mouth was a straight line of thin determination.

"Mr. Mason?" he said.

"Right."

"I'm Homer Gage. What did you wish to see me about?"

"Diana Douglas."

"What about her?"

"She's an employee of yours?"

"Yes. She is, but she's not here at the moment. Her brother was seriously injured in an automobile accident and I am afraid she is rather upset. If it's a matter of credit rating or integrity, I can assure you that she has a fine reputation."

"It's neither," Mason said. "I wanted to talk to you about her."

"Well, I'm here."

"All right," Mason said, "if you want to talk here, we'll talk here. I'm representing Miss Douglas. What was the idea of telling the Los Angeles police that she had embezzled twenty thousand dollars from this . . ."

Gage interrupted, throwing up his hands, palms outward. "Stop right there, Mr. Mason. We never said any such thing."

"Then you intimated it."

"Mr. Mason, this is hardly the time or the place to discuss a matter of this sort."

"What's wrong with the time?" Mason asked.

"Why . . . I hadn't anticipated . . . you didn't telephone . . . I had no warning."

"Did you need warning?"

"Not necessarily."

"Then what's wrong with the place?"

"It's public."

"You picked it," Mason reminded him.

Gage opened a gate in the counter. "Won't you please step into my private office, Mr. Mason?"

Mason followed him down a thick carpet where there

were further showcases on the sides, past two young
women, who very frankly stopped the work they were
doing to gawk at the lawyer as he walked past.

Gage held the door of his private office open, then,
when Mason had entered, said, "Please be seated, Mr.
Mason. I'm sorry you brought this up where the girls
in the outer office could hear it."

"You left me no choice," Mason said.

"Well, perhaps I didn't . . . I'm sorry. I didn't appreciate the importance of your visit."

"I hope you appreciate it now."

"Well, Mr. Mason, the fact remains that an audit of
the books shows that there is a very substantial shortage in our cash, and, of course, under the circumstances,
we wanted to check on any of our employees who are
absent."

"Diana Douglas was one?"

"Yes."

"Your uncle, Franklin Gage, is another?"

"Well, he's hardly an employee. He virtually owns
the business."

"And Edgar Douglas is another?"

"Yes. He's in the hospital with a fractured skull. He
has never regained consciousness since the accident. I'm
afraid the prognosis is not good."

"Did you check on him, too?" Mason asked.

"We were hardly in a position to check on him. You
can't question a man who is unconscious."

"So Diana Douglas was the only one you asked the
police to check on?"

"Now, Mr. Mason, you're getting the cart before the

horse. With a shortage of that sort showing up we quite naturally wanted to talk with Miss Douglas. That was our right. She's an employee of this company. We had assumed that she was absent from work because of the condition of her brother and was spending all of her time in the hospital with him, but inquiry disclosed that she had left rather suddenly for Los Angeles."

"And you asked the Los Angeles police to check on her?"

"The Los Angeles police were asked to try to get some information from her."

"You intimated that she might be an embezzler?"

"Certainly not, Mr. Mason. Don't try to put words in my mouth. We simply asked for a check-up."

"And how did you find out where she was staying in Los Angeles?"

"I'm afraid that's a confidential matter that I don't care to go into at the present time, Mr. Mason."

"All right," Mason said, "I just wanted you to know that I'm representing Miss Douglas; that we feel that her reputation has been damaged because she was accused of embezzlement, at least by inference, and because you asked the Los Angeles police to look her up. . . . Here is my card, Mr. Gage, and if you have any further matters to take up with Miss Douglas you can take them up with me."

"You mean she is finished working here?" Gage asked.

"That is something I'm not prepared to discuss," Mason said. "I am referring only to the case she has against you for defamation of character. I would suggest you get in touch with me if you have any further activities in mind."

"Come, come, Mr. Mason. There's no need to be belligerent. You don't need to come up here with a chip on your shoulder. Did you come up all the way from Los Angeles to tell us this?"

"Why not?" Mason asked.

"It seems so futile, so— Good heavens, we don't know where the money is. All we know is that there's a shortage."

"You're sure of that?"

"Apparently so. An amount of something over twenty thousand dollars seems to be missing from the cash."

"You keep an amount of that sort on hand in the form of ready cash?"

"Yes, indeed. We have a lot more than that."

"May I ask why?" Mason asked.

"I don't know why not," Gage said. "A lot of our deals are for cash, and a great many of them are made on weekends when the banks are closed."

"And on some of them you don't want any question of having left a backtrack?"

"No, no, no, it isn't that. It's simply that we've followed a policy of buying many times for cash and then, when the deal is completed, getting . . . well . . . establishing—"

"I'm afraid I don't understand," Mason interposed.

"It's rather difficult to understand, Mr. Mason, but there are various embargoes in various countries which must be—well, taken into account. For instance, in Mexico it is illegal to export ancient artifacts, yet there is a very brisk demand for such artifacts in this country."

"And these Mexican figurines have been smuggled out of Mexico?"

"I didn't say that, Mr. Mason. I was very careful *not* to say that. I was telling you something about the reasons that we have to have large supplies of cash in our business. There are certain questions we do not ask. And when you do not ask questions, cash does the talking."

"I'm afraid I don't understand," Mason said.

"Is it necessary that you should?"

"I think it is."

Gage flushed. "After all, Mr. Mason, I have explained to you as much of our business activities as I think is required under the circumstances."

"When you talk about using cash," Mason said, "in order to get figurines across the border, I take it that you are referring to bribery."

"Not at all," Gage said. "You're a lawyer. You should be able to put two and two together."

"Perhaps I have," Mason told him.

"Perhaps you put two and two together and came up with an entirely wrong answer," Gage warned.

"In that event," Mason told him, smiling affably, "you'll have a chance to explain in greater detail in court."

"Now, wait a minute, Mason, there's nothing to go to court about, and there's no reason for you and me to get at loggerheads."

Mason said nothing.

Gage took a deep breath. "Let me explain it this way, Mr. Mason. Mexico has an embargo on shipping ancient artifacts out of the country. On the other hand, there is no embargo in the United States on importing ancient artifacts. Therefore, if someone shows up with a station wagon full of figurines from Mexico, we don't have to determine at the time we complete the transaction whether the figurines are genuine or whether they are copies.

"You must realize that there's quite an industry in Mexico in copying ancient figurines and selling some of the copies to tourists, who quite frequently think they're getting a genuine prehistoric artifact."

"That still doesn't explain the cash," Mason said.

"Well," Gage went on, "put yourself in the position of the man who is driving the station wagon. He wants to sell the artifacts. He wants to get what he considers a good price for them. He knows how much he had to pay for them. He wants to make a profit. But when a man has a station wagon filled with figurines of this sort, it's only reasonable to suppose that he's in business. It isn't merely an isolated transaction.

"Under those circumstances he prefers to have no official record of the transaction. He prefers to deal on a cash-and-carry basis.

"Then there's the other end of things, the export of goods from Hong Kong where it is necessary to have a Certificate of Origin. Here again there are situations which require cold, hard cash, which is transferred by wire.

"Now, it's not necessary to make any more detailed explanation than that. We . . ."

Gage broke off as one of the secretaries entered the door.

"I beg your pardon," she said, "but Mr. Franklin Gage has just returned."

"Ask him to come in, please," Homer Gage said. "Tell him that Mr. Perry Mason, an attorney of Los Angeles, is here and that it may be we will have to consult our own legal department."

"Why don't you do that?" Perry Mason said. "I'd much prefer talking with an attorney."

"No, no, no, not yet. I simply wanted Mr. Franklin Gage to understand the situation. He . . . here he is now."

Mason turned. The tall, distinguished-looking gentleman who stood in the doorway wore an affable smile on the lower part of his face, but his eyes were appraising and unsmiling. They were eyes which were wide and round and somehow seemed to dominate the face.

He was in his late forties, wore rimless spectacles which seemed somehow to emphasize the rather wide eyes. The mouth was large, the lips rather thick, and the smile was that of a man who is accustomed to using suave tactics in getting what he wants out of life.

"Mr. Mason, Mr. Franklin Gage," Homer Gage said.

Mason stood up.

Franklin Gage gave him a hand which seemed cushioned with flesh, as though the man's body had built up a layer of insulation in the right hand.

"Ah, yes, Mr. Mason," Gage said, "I've heard a great deal about you. Your reputation is not confined to Los Angeles by any means. It's a pleasure to meet you. What can we do for you, Mr. Mason?"

Homer Gage was quick to answer that question. "Mr. Mason is calling about Diana Douglas," he said. "You'll remember she's been absent for the last three or four days.

"We weren't particularly busy at the time and I gave her some time off. Her brother was seriously injured in an automobile accident and has been unconscious."

"I understand he passed away early this morning," Mason said.

The two Gages exchanged glances.

"Good heavens!" Homer said.

"The poor kid," Franklin muttered sympathetically.

"I'm glad you told us," Homer Gage said.

Franklin Gage turned to his nephew. "The firm must send flowers, Homer."

"Certainly. I'll attend to that."

"And contact Diana and see if there's anything we can do. We must express our sympathies."

"I'm afraid Mr. Mason doesn't want us to have any direct contact with Diana," Homer Gage explained. "And even if he had no objections, I don't think it would be wise—not until we consult our lawyers."

"Nonsense!" Franklin Gage snapped. "We can certainly be guided by the humanities and plain decency."

"I think you'd better listen to Mr. Mason," Homer said.

"And why should that make any difference?" Franklin inquired, his voice now losing its tone of cordiality.

Homer rushed in with a hurried explanation. "Well, it seems that Diana Douglas made a quick trip to Los Angeles for some reason and somehow word got out that she had traveled under an assumed name.

"Then Stewart Garland, in checking the cash, said that there seemed to be quite a discrepancy—a rough estimate fixed this discrepancy at some twenty thousand dollars. Quite naturally, I wanted to find out about it and I wanted to interrogate Diana Douglas."

"You mean you interrogated her about the cash shortage?" Franklin Gage asked.

"Well, not directly," Homer said. "I may have acted rather hastily, but when I found she was registered at a hotel under an assumed name, I asked a very close friend of mine on the police force what to do about it and he said he'd arrange to have her interrogated by some friends of his in the Los Angeles Police Department.

"Mr. Mason seems to feel that what we did amounted to an accusation of embezzlement against her and constituted a defamation of character."

"Tut, tut," Franklin Gage said to Homer, "you shouldn't have jumped at conclusions. A lot of people have access to that cash drawer—the way we do business, you know. I, myself, had ten thousand dollars which I took from the cash drawer in order to complete a deal I was working on. Unfortunately, the deal fell through. I returned the cash a few minutes ago."

"That would seem to leave us with a shortage of only ten thousand dollars then," Homer Gage said, his manner greatly deflated.

"You can't tell if there's been any shortage until you check everything," the older man replied. "You know how that cash vault is. We keep large sums there and whenever any of the executives need money they simply take out what they need and then leave a note stating what they have taken out. And sometimes those notes aren't up-to-date. That is, if a man's in a hurry he won't bother to leave a note.

"In my case I was negotiating for a deal which, unfortunately, fell through. I took out ten thousand dollars and didn't leave any note stating I had done so. I had no idea that there was going to be all this talk of embezzlement. . . . The way we're organized, Homer, you should have waited until you got all of us together before you even had any idea of embezzlement or let any talk of that sort get started."

"I'm sorry, but Diana Douglas used an assumed name, went to Los Angeles, and registered in a hotel as Diana Deering. Under those circumstances I felt that we—"

"How did you find out about all this?" Franklin Gage asked.

"Well, frankly, I didn't find out about it," Homer Gage said, now quite apparently on the defensive and somewhat flustered. "I wanted to ask Diana about the cash and whether she had any slips that had been taken from the cash safe which she intended to post. . . . Well, I found she wasn't in her apartment. She wasn't at the hospital with her brother, although she had been there faithfully for some two or three hours right after the accident. Then she seemed to have disappeared.

"Well, I had this friend on the police force and I asked him how a man would go about locating a young woman under those circumstances and he said he'd run down a couple of leads.

"Well, of course, he used common sense, something which I could have done if I'd only thought of it. He knew that Diana was concerned about her brother, so he went to the hospital, interrogated the telephone operator, and found that calls had been coming in regularly from Los Angeles to find out about Edgar Douglas' condition. A number had been left to be notified if there was any change. The officer found that number was the number of the Willatson Hotel in Los Angeles and that a Diana Deering had put in the calls. By checking her description he soon had it pretty well established that Diana Deering was Diana Douglas, so then he suggested that it would be a good plan to question her because—well, you can see the position I was in."

"I'm not going to make any comment at this time," Franklin Gage said, "but Diana Douglas has been a very loyal employee and I have the utmost confidence in her integrity. I'm sorry that Mr. Mason has adopted the attitude there has been any defamation of character. I also feel that we had better check up rather carefully on that cash situation before we talk about *any* shortage. . . . You will understand, Mr. Mason, that at times there is as much as a hundred thousand dollars in our cash safe.'

Mason raised his eyebrows.

"I know that seems large to you," Franklin Gage

went on, "but it seems small to us because this is a very unusual type of business.

"This isn't like dealing in automobiles where there is a registration number and a pink slip. In this business the person who has possession of the articles is to all intents and purposes the owner—unless, of course, he has stolen the articles—and that is a chance we have to take.

"However, we have a regular clientele with whom we do business, and we have been very fortunate in dealing in property which was not stolen."

"But smuggled?" Mason asked.

"I wouldn't know," Franklin Gage said, shaking his head. "I wouldn't want to know. And, of course, smuggling is only a minor crime. There are embargoes against exportation. If a shrewd operator ships a dozen figurines out of Mexico without alarming the Mexican authorities, and then presents them at the United States border as copies which he has picked up for a nominal consideration in a Tijuana curio store, nobody is going to bother about it because there *are* curio stores selling copies of ancient figurines.

"Then when they get to this country, if it should turn out that the figurines are actually genuine, ancient figurines, we certainly aren't going to ask how it happened that they were released from the embargo in Mexico. We simply say, 'How much?' And if the price is right and if we are satisfied as to the quality of the merchandise, we close the transaction."

"Then these ancient figurines in your display windows are copies?" Mason asked.

Franklin Gage shook his head. "We don't deal in copies, Mr. Mason. We deal in genuine, authentic articles."

"But they come across the border as copies?" Mason asked.

"We have no idea how they come across the border, Mr. Mason. . . .

"Now, may I say that we are genuinely concerned about Diana's misfortune, the loss of her brother. I know that they were very close. I take it that this is a poor time to communicate with her, but, after the funeral, Mr. Mason . . . I think you will agree with us that this whole discussion should be postponed until after the funeral?

"Personally, I don't see how any good can come of trying to intensify the feeling of grief, on the one hand, or of injured feelings on the other. Mr. Mason, I ask you please, as a favor to the company, as a personal favor, to hold this matter in abeyance for a few days. This is the end of the week and, as you say, Diana's brother has passed away. That will mean funeral arrangements, and the poor girl has— Homer, see if you can get her on the phone and ask her if she wants any money. Ask her if she needs an advance."

"Don't try it today," Mason said. "I have advised her to take sedation and shut off the telephone."

"Yes, yes, yes, I see," Franklin Gage said, "and, of course, tomorrow is Saturday, but— I think it might be a little better, Homer, if you had one of the other girls in the office—surely someone must know her intimately and have a friendship with her, someone who could ring up in a few hours and express our sympathy in a perfectly natural way."

Homer Gage shook his head. "Not Diana. She's something of a loner as far as the others are concerned, but I'll see what I can do."

Franklin Gage arose and again held out his flesh-cushioned hand to the lawyer. "So nice to have met you, Mr. Mason, and thank you so much for dropping in to tell us what you had in mind. I am quite certain that it won't be necessary for us to adopt any adversary position—not that I agree with you in any way, but—well, we'll work out something somewhere along the line.

"And please don't get the idea that we are engaged in an unusual type of business. I can assure you that every importing and exporting business these days has problems, Mr. Mason, and I think everyone has contacts."

"What do you mean, contacts?" Mason asked.

"Well, brokers," Franklin Gage said with a wave of his hand. "You know, Mr. Mason, we don't give money to every Tom, Dick, and Harry who shows up with a load of curios. But we have certain people with whom we deal, and those people, in turn, deal with other people and . . . well, it's not at all unusual for me to walk out of here, picking up five, ten, or perhaps fifteen thousand dollars in cash and contacting one of our brokers who will have a shipment of curios that we feel we can dispose of at a profit—Mexican figurines, carved ivories, or good jade.

"We know that the broker is only a middleman, and, of course, he is making a profit on the deal. We try to see that his profit is not exorbitant, but, on the other hand, we want him to make a fair profit because in this business everyone has to make a fair profit. . . . Well, you can understand how it is."

"I see," Mason said.

Homer Gage did not offer to shake hands. He stood somewhat aloof and dignified.

Franklin Gage held the door open for Mason. "Thank you again for coming in, Mr. Mason. It's nice that you felt free to come and explain the situation to us. I feel that it can be worked out. Good day, Mr. Mason."

"Good day," Mason said.

The lawyer walked across the office and, on his way out, paused momentarily at the counter to look at a piece of the carved ivory which claimed his attention. A small slip of folded paper had been placed by the carved ivory figure. The slip of paper had Mason's name typed on it.

Mason leaned forward to study the figure more closely. As he did so his right hand unostentatiously closed over the paper. When he straightened he placed the folded paper in the right-hand side pocket of his coat.

Mason went through the gate to the outer display room and paused again to look at some of the figurines in the outer cases.

"They're really very beautiful," the girl at the switchboard said, smiling at him.

"Indeed they are," Mason said. "They grow on you."

The lawyer left the office, walked out to the corridor,

and halfway to the elevator removed the small piece
of paper from his pocket. A typewritten message was in
his hand when he unfolded the paper.

The message read:

> Don't let them pull the wool over your eyes.
> Diana is on the level and tops. There are
> things going on here that they don't want you
> to know about. Be sure to protect Diana.

The message was unsigned.

Mason folded the typewritten slip of paper, put it
back into his pocket, went to his hotel, and checked
out.

Chapter Eleven

ON MONDAY morning Mason fitted a key in the lock of his private office and swung back the door.

"Well, hello, stranger!" Della Street said.

Mason smiled. "It isn't *that* bad!"

"Pretty close to it, what with running up and down to San Francisco and working with detectives. What do you know?"

"Not a darn thing," Mason said, "except that this Diana Douglas is a problem. I feel like throwing her out."

"Why don't you?"

"Well," Mason said, "I have a professional obligation."

"She's lied to you all the way along the line," Della Street said. "And when she hasn't been lying, she's tried to conceal things."

"I know," Mason said, "but the poor kid certainly was all wrapped up in her brother."

"The one that had the automobile accident?"

"He died early Friday morning," Mason said. "I guess the funeral is this morning. I told Diana to take some sleeping pills Friday; to go to sleep and forget the whole mess."

"And you went to see the Escobar Import and Export Company?"

"I met a couple of very interesting men," Mason said. "I'd like to know something about the inside operation of that company. I met Homer Gage and Franklin Gage and there you have a couple of real characters."

"Smooth?"

"Puzzling. . . . Homer Gage has to control himself with an effort every once in a while. Franklin Gage is synthetically suave. He gives you the impression of having tried all of his life to keep from showing his real feelings. When he shakes hands with you you feel there's a cushion of flesh on his hand, a sort of sponge-rubber insulation that he uses to keep any magnetic current from penetrating."

"From him to you?" Della asked.

Mason thought for a moment, then smiled and said, "Both ways. . . . We're getting into a deep subject, Della, but somehow when you shake hands with a man you can tell a lot about him from his grip. There's a certain magnetic something you can feel."

"I know," she said. "Some hands are firm and sincere and others are—well, sort of evasive; it's hard to describe."

Mason was thoughtful. "Shaking hands is a peculiar

custom. It consists in clasping a part of two bodies together so that a vibration or magnetism or whatever you want to call it is exchanged from one to the other. . . . Well, we'd better go to work."

Della Street shook her head. "You had two appointments for this morning, and when I didn't hear from you Friday afternoon I canceled them."

"I should have let you know," Mason said, "but I got up there and had this session with the Escobar Import and Export Company and I had a peculiar experience."

"What?"

"One of the stenographers left this note with my name on it beside a piece of carved ivory I had been looking at."

"Oh, oh," Della Street said. "So that's why you stayed over in San Francisco Friday night!"

Mason grinned. "It wasn't that kind of a note. Take a look."

The lawyer took the note from his notebook. Della Street looked at it, said, "I think it was done on an electric typewriter. Did you notice which of the secretaries had electric typewriters?"

"I didn't," Mason said. "I was noticing the decorations in the office—figurines, carved ivories, jade. They must have had half a million dollars' worth of stuff on display."

"Did they offer you anything at a discount?"

"Wholesale only," Mason said thoughtfully. "I'd like to know something about who their customers are and

I'd like to know a lot more about where they get their stuff. . . . You say you canceled all my appointments for this morning?"

"That's right. They weren't important, and I rang up Friday afternoon and canceled."

Mason said, "After I got out of the Import and Export Company I went out to Fisherman's Wharf and had a good crab lunch—or I guess you'd call it dinner —and then went down to the airport. . . . Friday afternoon at a San Francisco airport. I was lucky to get home at all. I didn't get in until five-fifteen and then I didn't want to bother you. . . . I'm going down to Paul Drake's office and see if our stakeout has heard anything."

"Our stakeout?"

"Stella Grimes," Mason said, "the operative who's registered under the name of Diana Deering at the Willatson Hotel. Somehow I have an idea we may be a bit behind on developments.

"For your information Franklin Gage seemed to adopt a rather casual attitude toward a shortage of twenty thousand dollars. Actually it was only ten thousand, because Franklin had taken out ten thousand to use in a business deal that he hadn't consummated, and he had put the money back when he came in the office Friday morning."

"But he reported what he had done?"

"Yes, as soon as his nephew told him there was a shortage."

"Well, that was opportune," Della Street said.

Mason nodded. "The way they keep their cash is certainly cool and casual. I have an idea that Franklin Gage would a lot rather absorb a reasonable loss than have the matter come into court where he would be cross-examined about the reason they keep such a large amount of cash on hand and what they do with it. . . . There could be an income-tax angle there, too . . . and I'm willing to bet there's a lot of customs regulations that are being by-passed."

"You think they're smuggling?"

"I think people with whom they deal are smuggling, and there's an atmosphere of complete irregularity about the whole thing. . . . Some of those art objects they have on display are *really* beautiful. . . . I'm going down and have a chat with Paul Drake for a minute, Della. I think he's in this morning. Then I'll come back and get my nose ready for the grindstone."

"You have three rather important appointments this afternoon," she reminded him.

"Okay," Mason said, "I'll take a quick look; then back to the salt mines. . . . I guess Edgar Douglas' funeral is this morning. After that we may hear from Diana. And then again we may never hear from her again. I have an idea our Franklin Gage will be at the funeral, and he may tell Diana the whole embezzlement idea was a false alarm.

"Diana certainly looked a wreck. She had taken a plane up from Los Angeles, gone to the hospital, was with her brother when he died about three o'clock in the morning; then had to make funeral arrangements and meet me at the Escobar Import and Export Company at ten-thirty and—say, wait a minute, I told her to get a cashier's check. She had it for me."

Mason took the leather wallet from his inside coat pocket, pulled out several papers, and said, "Well, here it is. A cashier's check made by the Farmers' Financial Bank of San Francisco to Diana Douglas as trustee in an amount of five thousand dollars. She may have cut corners with us, Della, but she followed instructions on that check at a time when her heart must have been torn to ribbons. She was really fond of that brother of hers. I guess she's sort of been a mother to him as well as a sister. . . . If anything turns up in the next ten minutes, I'll be down at Paul Drake's office."

"No hurry," Della Street said. "I'll call if there's anything important."

Mason walked down the corridor to the offices of the Drake Detective Agency, said hello to the girl at the switchboard, and jerked his thumb in the direction of Paul Drake's office.

She smiled in recognition, nodded, and said, "He's in. He's on the phone at the moment. Go on down."

Mason opened the spring-locked gate in the partition which divided the waiting room from the offices and walked down the long corridor, flagged by little offices in which Drake's operatives made out their reports, until he came to Drake's office.

Paul Drake was sitting in his little cubbyhole behind a desk on which were several telephones. He was just completing a telephone conversation when Mason opened the door.

The detective indicated a chair and said, "Hi, Perry. This is intended as a place of command from which to direct multitudinous activities, not as a place of consultation."

Mason settled himself in the chair. "What have you got on those phones—a hot line to police headquarters?"

"Darned near," Drake said. "We handle a lot of the stuff at the switchboard, but on delicate assignments when we have cars cruising with telephones in them, there are lots of times when there just isn't time to go through a switchboard. I give the operatives an unlisted number. They can call me direct and be absolutely certain that they're going to get me here."

"But suppose you're not here?" Mason asked.

"Then there's a signal on the switchboard and the switchboard can pick it up, but I'm usually here. When you run a job like this you have to sit on top of it, and that's particularly true with men who are cruising with cars that have telephones. . . . What's on your mind, Perry?"

"This thirty-six-twenty-four-thirty-six case," Mason said. "Diana Douglas is the sort of girl who will go to a doctor to get medicine for the flu; then go home, take the advice of the janitor, take two aspirins with a hot lemonade, and throw out the doctor's medicine. Then a friend will drop in who'll tell her that what she needs is a lot of vitamin C and whiskey; so she'll take five hundred units of vitamin C and a hot toddy. Then somebody will tell her she needs hot tea and quinine and she'll take that. Then when the doctor comes to see how she's getting along she'll push the whiskey bottle and the teapot under the bed so he won't know she's taken anything on her own and say, 'Doctor, I feel terrible!' "

Drake grinned. "You're just describing human nature, Perry. What's she done now?"

"Nothing," Mason said. "She was very, very much attached to her brother who was in that automobile accident. He passed away early Friday morning. But up to that point our little Miss Douglas did all kinds of things, or rather didn't do all kinds of things. She was supposed to go up to San Francisco with me on the plane, but she didn't make it. She said she had a feeling that someone was following her.

"Ordinarily I'd have accepted that as the gospel truth, but in view of her record I'm inclined to doubt it. Anyway, Paul, we'd better get our double out of the Willatson Hotel, and then we'll sit tight on the case for a while."

"Can you tell me any more about it without violating ethics?" Drake asked.

Mason shook his head. "Remember, Paul, I was your client in this case and all that you found out about Diana Douglas came from the detective work you did.

"Let's give Stella Grimes a jingle. Tell her to pack up and come on home."

Drake picked up the telephone, said, "Call the Willatson Hotel and get Room Seven-sixty-seven for me."

A moment later he said, "Hello, Stella. I guess the job's over. You'd better pack up and— What's that? . . . Are you sure. . . ?

"Hold on a minute, Stella."

Drake looked up at Mason and said, "Stella thinks there's something funny going on. She went out to get breakfast and a man followed her. She's pretty certain there's a man on duty at the end of the seventh-floor corridor keeping an eye on the elevator."

Mason looked at his watch. "Tell her we're on our way down there, Paul."

"Gosh, Perry, I can't get away. I can send an operative if—"

"I can handle it," Mason said. "I just thought you might like to go along. I'm free this morning, and if our friend Moray Cassel has got one of his little pimp friends waiting to throw a scare into the occupant of Room Seven-sixty-seven, it'll be my great pleasure to tell the guy where he gets off."

"Take it easy, Perry," Drake warned. "Some of these guys are vicious."

"I'm vicious myself," Mason said, "when some pimp starts shoving a woman around."

Mason left Drake's office, said to the girl at Drake's switchboard, "Ring my office, will you please, and tell Della Street that I'm out on an errand for an hour, that I'll be back then."

"An errand?" the girl at the switchboard asked. "Just that?"

"Well," Mason said, grinning, "you can tell her it's an errand of mercy. Also, if she gets inquisitive, tell her that I've had to sit in a position of command and let the troops do the fighting for so long that I'm getting rusty. I think I need to get out on the firing line myself."

"You want me to tell her that?"

"On second thought," Mason said, "you'd better not. Tell her that I'll be back in an hour."

The lawyer took the elevator to the ground floor, picked up a taxicab, gave the address of the Willatson Hotel, went up to the seventh floor, and noticed a man with a hammer and chisel doing some work at the end of the hall. Otherwise he saw no one.

The lawyer walked down to Room 767, tapped gently on the door, and said, "Oh, Diana."

Stella Grimes opened the door. "Come in, Mr. Mason. And don't ever give me any more assignments like this one."

Mason said, "You mean you're alarmed because somebody is following you?"

"Heavens, no," she said, "I'm bored stiff. Did you ever sit in a hotel room hour after hour waiting for something to happen and nothing happens? You turn on the radio and have a choice of two stations. You listen to a lot of inane jabbering until you get tired. You move from one chair to another. You have meals served in your room, and don't leave the phone because you're afraid that someone may want you on something important. You don't dare to call up anyone because you don't want to tie the telephone line up in case the boss wants you. I'll bet I've slept enough in the last two or three days to last me for a month. I went out this morning for the first time in days. The chambermaid was getting suspicious, so I phoned the office switchboard that I'd be out for forty-five minutes and went out for some air.

"Next time I hope you can give me a job that's got some action to it."

"Where you'll have a chance to use your official bra?" Mason asked.

She smiled and said, "I never have had to actually *use* it. I've pulled it a couple of times when the going got tough. I . . ." She broke off as knuckles sounded on the door.

"Don't tell me nothing ever happens," Mason said. "We're calling things off too soon. Even money that's our friend Moray Cassel."

"And if he finds me here again?"

"Look guilty," Mason said. "Be the party of the second part in a surreptitious assignation. . . . And then be very careful. The guy will want to sign you up as a part of his stable of call girls."

Knuckles sounded heavily on the door again. Mason nodded to Stella Grimes. "It's your room," he said.

She crossed over and opened the door.

Two men who were standing on the threshold pushed their way into the room. They were not the same officers who had called previously.

"Is this your credit card?" one of the men said. "Did you lose it?"

He handed Stella Grimes a BankAmericard credit card, then saw Mason and said, "Who's your friend?"

"Better ask your questions one at a time," Stella Grimes said. "Which comes first?"

One of the men turned belligerently to Perry Mason, said, "Who are you?"

The other man kept pushing the credit card at

Stella Grimes. "All right," he said, "*is* it your credit card or *isn't* it?"

Stella Grimes glanced at Mason, said, "This seems to be a BankAmericard credit card issued to Diana Douglas."

"Is it yours or isn't it?"

"I . . ."

"Don't answer that," Mason said, his voice sharp as the crack of a whip.

"Now, just a minute, Mac," the man said, "you're sticking your nose into a . . ."

"Wait a minute, wait a minute, Bill," the second man warned, "this is a lawyer. I recognize him now. This is Perry Mason."

"What the hell are you doing here?" the man asked.

"What are *you* doing here?" Mason countered.

"We're trying to find out whether this credit card is the property of this young woman."

"A credit card made out to Diana Douglas?" Mason asked.

"That's right. Diana Douglas."

Mason, suddenly thoughtful, said, "If you are investigating any crime it is incumbent that you warn the suspect and tell her of her constitutional rights."

"All right," the man said, "we're plain-clothes police. Homicide squad. Here are our credentials."

He took a leather folder from his pocket, opened it, and displayed a badge and an I.D. card. "Now then, young lady, you're entitled to remain silent if you want to. If you answer questions anything you say may be used against you. You're entitled to have an attorney at all stages of the proceedings."

"She has an attorney," Mason said. "I'm her lawyer. Now, tell her the specific crime of which she is accused."

"She isn't accused of anything yet," the man said, "but we're following a hot lead. For your information we want to question her about the murder of Moray Cassel, who lived in the Tallmeyer Apartments in Apartment Nine-o-six. Now then, you want to talk or don't you?"

"Just a minute," Mason said, "let me think."

"You'd better think fast," the man said. "We're not out to frame anything on anybody, but unless this young lady can explain what her credit card was doing in the apartment with the murdered man she's in trouble. If she can explain it, we're perfectly willing to listen and to check on any leads she gives us."

Mason said, "When was this man, Cassel, murdered?"

"Now, *you're* asking questions," the man said. "We're the ones who are asking questions, and we want some answers fast."

Mason said, "If you want some answers fast, you'd better grab that man at the end of the hall who's working down there with a hammer and chisel and find out where *he* fits into the picture."

The man grinned and said, "Don't worry, buddy, he's one of our men. We've had this room under surveillance since early this morning, hoping that somebody would come in. We were sort of looking for a male accomplice. You triggered our visit."

Mason said to Stella Grimes, "Show him your credentials, Stella."

Stella Grimes reached for her purse.

"Now, take it easy, you two," one of the officers said, "nothing fast or there's going to be a *lot* of trouble. Just hand *me* your purse, sister, and I'll look in it first."

She handed him the purse. He looked through it, then handed it back to her and said, "Okay, pull out your credentials."

Stella Grimes pulled out her license as a private detective.

Mason said, "For your information, I'm baiting a trap myself. Stella Grimes is a private detective, an employee of the Drake Detective Agency, and she's been here masquerading as Diana Deering from San Francisco."

The officer regarded the credentials thoughtfully. Then said, "And Diana Deering is an alias for Diana Douglas?"

"I didn't say that," Mason said.

"You didn't have to."

There was a moment of silence. Mason said, "I believe I have a professional obligation as an attorney and as a citizen to cooperate with the police in investigating serious charges.

"Since you apparently thought this was Diana Douglas I advised you as to her true identity and occupation. That's as far as we're going."

"Why did you want a double?" the officer asked.

"No comment."

"Anything to do with Moray Cassel?"

"No comment."

"Now, look," the officer said, "if this Diana Douglas happens to be your client—oh, oh, that's the angle, Bill. . . . Or is it?"

The officer addressed as Bill disgustedly pushed the credit card back in his pocket. "Well," he said, "we've tipped our hand now."

The other officer said to Mason, "Any attempt on your part to communicate with Diana Douglas will be considered as a hostile act by law-enforcement officers and may make you an accessory."

Mason said to Stella Grimes, "Take the phone, Stella, put through a call for Diana Douglas."

The officer called Bill threw a shoulder block and pushed her out of the way of the telephone. He picked up the phone, said to the operator, "This is a police emergency call. Get me police headquarters in San Francisco immediately."

The second officer stood guard, protecting the telephone.

A moment later the officer at the telephone said, "This is the Los Angeles police, Bill Ardley talking. We want you to pick up a Diana Douglas for questioning. She works for the Escobar Import and Export Company. She has a BankAmerica credit card issued in her name. . . . You folks gave us a tip that she was in Los Angeles at the Willatson Hotel, registered as Diana Deering. That's a bum steer. She's probably in San Francisco at the present time. Pick her up for questioning, and then notify us in Room Seven-sixty-seven at the Willatson Hotel. . . . You got my name okay?

This is Bill Ardley of— Oh, you know me, eh? . . .
That's right, I worked with you a year ago on that
Smith case. . . . Well, that's fine. I'll appreciate anything you can do. Get on this immediately, will you?
And when you pick her up ask her first rattle out of the
box where her BankAmerica credit card is. If she says
she lost it, find out when she lost it. . . . Okay. G'by."

The officer depressed the connecting lever with his
finger rapidly several times until he got the hotel operator. Then he said, "This is the Los Angeles police,
operator. Put this phone out of service until we stop by
the switchboard and give you instructions to the contrary. We'll take all incoming calls. No outgoing calls,
no matter who makes the call, unless it's identified as
being police business. You got that? Okay."

The officer hung up the telephone, settled himself
spraddle-legged across one of the straight-back chairs.
"Okay, my lawyer friend," he said, "now suppose *you*
start doing a little talking."

"On the other hand, suppose I don't," Mason said.

"We wouldn't like that," the officer said.

"Start not liking it, then," Mason said. "I'm leaving."

"Oh, no, you aren't! Not for a while."

"Do I take it," Mason asked, "that you're intending
to hold us here?"

The officer smiled affably, nodded. "I'm going to do
the best I can."

"Now, that might not be very smart," Mason said.
"If you put me under arrest you're laying yourself open
for suit for unlawful arrest, and this young woman is—"

"Take it easy," the officer interrupted. "I'm making this play for your own good. You may thank me for it later—both of you."

"That credit card," Mason said, "is that a clue in the murder?"

The officer said, "What do you think of the Dodgers' chances this year?"

"Pretty good," Mason said.

"Now then," the officer went on, "we'd like to know when was the last time you saw Diana Douglas, what you talked about at that time, and what you told her."

"You know I can't betray the confidence of a client," Mason said. "What do *you* think of the Dodgers' chances?"

"Pretty good," the officer said. He turned to Stella Grimes. "You don't have any professional immunity," he said. "You're a private detective, you have a license. You have to cooperate with the police. What brought you here?"

Stella Grimes looked helplessly at Mason.

"He's right," Mason said, "tell him."

She said, "Mr. Mason telephoned the Drake Detective Agency where I work and asked for me to come over here and go under the name of Diana Deering, and if anyone asked for me at the desk using the code figures thirty-six twenty-four thirty-six I was to answer."

"Anybody come?" the officer asked.

Again she looked at Mason.

"Tell him," Mason said. "You're a witness. He's investigating a homicide."

She said, "A man came here and acted rather peculiarly."

"In what way?"

"He acted as if he might be trying to put across some sort of a blackmail scheme."

"And what did you tell him?"

She said, "I didn't tell him anything. I let Mr. Mason do the talking."

"And what did Mr. Mason tell him?"

"I wouldn't know. I left the room. I got a signal to act as Mr. Mason's girl friend who had been enjoying a rendezvous in the hotel and I went over to him, kissed him, and walked out."

"Leaving Mason and this man alone?"

"Yes."

"What did the man look like?"

"He was about—well, in his middle thirties. He had slick, black hair and was—well groomed. His trousers were creased. His shoes were shined, his nails manicured."

The officer frowned. "Did that man give you any name?" he asked.

Again she looked at Mason.

Mason nodded.

"He said his name was Cassel."

"I'll be damned," the officer muttered.

There was silence for several seconds. Then the officer said, "So, you left the room and left Mason and this man alone here?"

"That's right."

"Where did you go?"

"Tell him," Mason said.

She said, "Mr. Mason gave me a coded signal to follow the man who left here. I found it was absurdly easy. He had parked his Cadillac automobile right in front of the entrance and had tipped the doorman to take care of it for him. I got the license number of the automobile. It was WVM five-seven-four. I hopped in a taxicab, and when this man came out and got in his Cadillac automobile I told the cab driver to follow."

"And you followed him?"

"Yes."

"To where?"

"To the Tallmeyer Apartments."

"Then what?"

"Then I used a few evasive tactics so I didn't lay myself wide open to the taxi driver so he could pick up a good fee by tipping off the driver of the Cadillac that he had been followed."

"Then what?"

"Then I came back and reported."

The officer looked at Mason. "Take it from there, Mason," he said.

Mason said, "I'm an attorney, acting in a professional capacity, representing a client. I have no information in which you would be interested except that I have no comment on what this young woman has said."

"But," the officer said, "you immediately traced the license number of that automobile, did you not?"

"No comment."

"And found out it was registered to Moray Cassel in Apartment Nine-o-six at the Tallmeyer Apartments?"

"No comment."

"And," the officer went on, "if it appears that you passed that information on to Diana Douglas we've got just about the most perfect, airtight murder case you ever encountered. Even the great Mason isn't going to beat this one."

"Still no comment," Mason said.

The officer took out a pack of cigarettes, selected one, offered a smoke to Stella Grimes, then to Mason, and last to his brother officer.

"Well," he said, "we seem to have uncovered a live lead."

They smoked in silence, the officer quite evidently thinking over the information Stella Grimes had given him.

There was more desultory conversation for some twenty minutes. Then the phone rang. The officer answered the phone. A slow smile spread over his face.

"Okay," he said.

He turned to Mason and waved toward the door. "You and this young woman are as free as the air," he said. "Go any place you want."

Mason held the door open for Stella Grimes. "Bring your things," he said. "We've finished. That means they've picked her up in San Francisco."

Chapter Twelve

PERRY MASON sat on the edge of the seat of the taxicab counting the minutes until the driver reached his office building. Then he tossed the driver a five-dollar bill, said, "Keep the change, cabbie. Thanks for speeding it up as much as possible."

The lawyer sprinted across the foyer of the building into the elevator, then hurried down the hallway to his office.

"Well, hello!" Della Street said as he made an explosive entrance into his private office. "What's the rush?"

"Heard anything from Diana Douglas?" Mason asked.

She shook her head.

"Any collect call from San Francisco?"

Again she shook her head.

Mason sighed his relief, picked up the telephone, said to Gertie, "If any call comes in from San Francisco reversing the charges, I'll take it. Put the call right through to me."

The lawyer settled back in the swivel chair at his desk, took a deep breath, and said, "If we don't hear within the next fifteen minutes, we'll call the San Francisco police and make a demand on them, and if that doesn't do the trick we'll start a writ of *habeas corpus* in San Francisco."

"What's happened?"

"They've arrested Diana Douglas."

"On the embezzlement?"

Mason shook his head. "The embezzlement is a minor matter," he said, "although they *may* try to arrest her on the embezzlement so they can hold her up there in the hope that she'll talk. If they do that I'm going to have to get right back to San Francisco in a hurry. . . . The charge they are putting against her is the murder of Moray Cassel."

"What!" Della exclaimed.

Mason nodded. "Somebody got into Moray Cassel's apartment, killed him, and made an exit."

"And the police think it was Diana Douglas?"

Mason nodded.

"When was this done?" she asked.

"There's something of a problem. The police will probably try to show it was done Thursday afternoon. The body probably wasn't discovered until today. That's going to make a ticklish problem with experts giving various opinions, contradicting each other, and all of the stuff that goes with it."

Della Street was thoughtful for a moment, "And our client was to have met you on the plane Thursday night at six twenty-seven and didn't show up?"

Mason nodded.

"Do you suppose there's any chance she could have been— But no, she isn't that kind of a girl."

"How do you know she isn't?" Mason asked.

"You have ideas?" Della Street asked.

Mason said thoughtfully, "When I saw her in San Francisco she told me that when she got to the airport she didn't have her credit card which she intended to use to pay for her ticket. Then she remembered that I had ordered two tickets charged to my account, so she picked up one of those tickets and said she'd adjust with me."

"And?" Della Street asked, as Mason hesitated.

"And," Mason said, "two officers from homicide showed up at the Willatson Hotel, barged in on Stella Grimes, shoved a BankAmerica credit card made out to Diana Douglas at her, and asked her to please identify the card."

"Did she?"

Mason said, "I stepped into the picture, told her to keep quiet, and then it suddenly developed we were playing for much bigger stakes than the embezzlement. This was a murder investigation and I didn't dare to carry on the deception any longer. So I had Stella Grimes identify herself to the officers, and then they rushed through a call to San Francisco as soon as they got the sketch and left orders to pick up Diana Douglas immediately on a charge of homicide."

"And you're expecting she'll telephone you?"

Mason nodded. "If she'll just follow instructions for once, keep her head, and keep her mouth shut—but they're going to bring her down here and really try to work her over."

"And so we enter into the picture?" Della Street asked.

"We enter into the picture," Mason said. "We—"

He broke off as his phone rang, and, motioning to Della to monitor the conversation in shorthand, Mason picked up the receiver and said, "Perry Mason talking."

A harsh voice said, "You're attorney for Diana Douglas, an employee of Escobar Import and Export Company?"

"Right."

"She's under arrest and is asking for an opportunity to communicate with you. We've given her that opportunity."

"Put her on," Mason said.

"It's a collect call," the official voice reminded.

"Quite right," Mason said.

A moment later Diana's frightened voice said, "Mr. Mason, I don't understand. They're charging me, they claim that—"

"Shut up," Mason said. "Don't talk. Listen!"

"Yes, Mr. Mason."

Mason said, "They're going to charge you with the murder of Moray Cassel. They will offer to take you before a magistrate in San Francisco before taking you to Los Angeles. I want you brought down here. Keep your mouth shut. Don't say anything to anyone about anything. Just use two words, 'No comment', and then add, 'I answer no questions. I make no statements except in the presence of my attorney, Perry Mason.' Can you remember that?"

"Yes."

"Can you do it?"

"I think so."

"Let me talk to the officer in charge," Mason said.

A moment later the official voice came on the line once more.

Mason said, "I'm attorney for Diana Douglas. I have instructed her to make no statement except in my presence. We waive any hearing in San Francisco in favor of a hearing before a magistrate in Los Angeles County. We make no objection to being transported from San Francisco to Los Angeles. Aside from that we make no stipulations, no admissions, no concessions, and as attorney for Miss Douglas I insist that I be present at all interviews and at all questioning. I wish to be notified the moment she arrives in Los Angeles."

"If you'd let us talk things over with her, we might be able to straighten this out," the officer said. "We don't want to bring her down to Los Angeles unless there's some real reason for it. If she can explain some of the circumstantial evidence in the case, and I certainly hope she can because she's a very nice young woman who seems to have had a lot of trouble lately, we'll turn her loose."

"That's certainly nice of you," Mason said. "It's a wonderful line. It's caused a lot of people to talk themselves into prison. For your information, I have instructed Diana Douglas not to talk unless I am present, and I am instructing you not to interrogate her except in my presence. I don't want her interrogated by anybody unless I am there. I am making a record of this conversation so that any further attempts to get information from Miss Douglas will be a violation of her constitutional rights. I think you understand the situation."

"Well, as her attorney, will you explain certain things that we'd like to clear up?" the officer asked.

"I explain nothing," Mason said.

"Do you know when your client first noticed that her BankAmerica credit card was missing?"

Mason laughed into the telephone.

"What's so funny?" the officer at the other end of the line asked.

"You are," Mason said, and hung up.

Chapter Thirteen

IN THE consultation room at the County Jail, Diana regarded Mason with tear-swollen eyes.

"Have you had any trouble with the police?" Mason asked.

"They've been wonderful to me," she said, "just so kind and considerate and— Mr. Mason, it wouldn't hurt to tell them certain things, would it?"

"What things?"

"Well, about finding the money and about Edgar and about why I put the ad in the paper and—"

"And where would you stop?" Mason asked.

"Well, I suppose I'd have to stop somewhere. I suppose you'd want me to."

"Of course," Mason said, "you wouldn't want to talk yourself right into the gas chamber. You'd want to stop sometime before you got there, but the trouble is you wouldn't know where to stop."

"Yes," she said, "I suppose I'd have to, but they've been so nice and considerate and—"

"Sure," Mason said, "that's part of the technique. With some people they're nice and considerate. With some women they're perfectly gentlemanly and fatherly. Then, if that doesn't work, they try the other tactic. They become hard-boiled and try all sorts of things.

"In recent years the courts have frowned on some of these police tactics, and the result is that they try to work up a case by getting the evidence rather than forcing the defendant to incriminate himself. But if anyone is willing to talk they're always willing to listen and many a person has talked himself right into the penitentiary, and I mean many an innocent person. He's made statements without knowing all of the facts."

"But I know all the facts," she said.

"Do you?"

"Yes."

"Who killed Moray Cassel?"

She winced at the question.

"Did you?" Mason asked.

"No."

Mason said, "Look here, Diana, you can be frank with me. I'm the only one you can be frank with. It's my duty to see that you have a defense whether you're innocent or guilty.

"Now then, you were to meet me on that six twenty-seven plane Thursday night. You didn't do it. I saw you the next morning and you had quite a story about having been followed by someone whom you couldn't shake off, someone who frightened you so you resorted to all sorts of evasive tactics and got there too late to catch the plane.

"Actually, you didn't even try to catch that plane. That story that you made up about someone following you was a lie to account for what you had done with your time.

"I gave you the information that the blackmailer was Moray Cassel. I gave you his address. You decided that I was never going to pay off a blackmailer and that might not be the thing that your brother wanted. So, you took it on yourself to second-guess my play. You took a taxicab to the Tallmeyer Apartments. You went up to see Moray Cassel. While you were up there something happened. You opened your purse, perhaps to take out a gun. When you opened your purse, your BankAmerica credit card fell out and you didn't miss it at the time.

"Later on you went to the airport. You wanted to buy your ticket to San Francisco and pay for it yourself, and that was when you missed your BankAmerica credit card for the first time.

"Now then, the police either know this much or surmise this much or can get evidence which will come pretty close to proving this much."

She shook her head.

"Yes, they can," Mason said. "The police are unbelievably clever. You have no idea what dogged footwork will accomplish in an investigation. They'll find the cab driver who took you to the Tallmeyer Apartments."

She gave a sudden, quick intake of her breath.

"Oh, oh," Mason said, "that hurt. . . . You little fool, do you mean that you took a cab directly to the Tallmeyer Apartments and didn't try to cover your tracks?"

"I was in a terrible hurry," she said. "I wanted to see him and then catch that plane with you. I thought I had time enough to pay him a quick visit and if . . . well, if . . . I was going to use my own judgment."

"In other words," Mason said, "if you felt that you could clean up the whole business with a five-thousand-dollar pay-off instead of putting that five thousand dollars into the bank and getting a check to yourself as trustee, you were going to pay him the five thousand dollars and try to make a deal with him by which your brother would be out of trouble."

"Well, yes . . ."

"Why didn't you do it?" Mason said.

"Because he was dead."

"Go on," Mason told her.

She said, "I got into the apartment house. It was one of these hotel-type apartment houses where they have a doorman on duty at the elevator, but he was busy parking a car for somebody and I slipped right on by him into the elevator. I went up to the ninth floor. I found apartment nine-o-six. I tapped on the door.

"Nothing happened, so I tapped again and when nothing happened I tried the knob. I don't know what in the world possessed me to do that but I did and the door opened and . . ."

"Just a minute," Mason said, "were you wearing gloves?"

"I . . . no."

Mason sighed and shook his head. "Go on," he said.

"I got in there and at first I didn't see him. I didn't see anybody, but I said, 'Who-whoo, is anybody home?' and walked in. And then I saw him lying there on his back on the bed. Oh, Mr. Mason, it was terrible, terrible. Everything was soaked in blood and . . ."

"Was he dead?" Mason asked.

She nodded.

"How do you know?"

"I picked up his hand and it was cold."

"Then what did you do?"

"I ran out."

"No, you didn't," Mason said. "You opened your purse. Why did you open your purse?"

"Heavens, I don't know, Mr. Mason. I . . . it's just . . . I suppose I was crying or something and wanted a handkerchief. . . . I can't begin to tell you how I felt. It was . . . I was almost nauseated."

Mason said, "You damn little liar. I have a notion to grab you by the shoulders and shake the truth out of you. Why did you open your purse?"

"I've told you, Mr. Mason. I've told you the truth."

Mason said, "You either opened your purse to take out a gun or to put a gun into it. Which was it?"

She looked at him with sullen resentment. "You always try to cross-examine me!"

"Because you always try to lie to me," Mason said. "Which was it?"

"I picked up the gun," she said.

"That's better," Mason told her. "Now, why did you pick up the gun?"

"Because it was Edgar's gun."

"How do you know it was?"

"I know it. He had a twenty-two revolver that he used to carry with him when he'd go out on his fishing trips on account of rattlesnakes and things of that sort. It had a polished wooden handle or grip, or whatever you call it, and a little piece was chipped out and . . ."

"Mr. Mason, it was Edgar's gun. I know it when I see it. Edgar always wanted to teach me to shoot, and I've shot that gun hundreds of times."

"So you picked up the gun and put it in your purse?" Mason said.

She nodded.

"And then what?"

"Then I tiptoed out of the room."

"And what did you do with the gun?"

"I'm all right on that, Mr. Mason. Nobody's ever going to find that gun. You can rest assured of that."

"They may not need to find it," Mason said.

"What do you mean?"

Mason said, "Every bullet which is fired through the barrel of a gun has certain distinctive striations or scratches that are made by peculiarities in the surface of the barrel. If the bullet that killed Moray Cassel was not deformed by striking bone and if the police can find where your brother had been target practicing, they can find some of the bullets which are embedded in a tree or a bank or whatever you used as a target. Then they can put those bullets in a comparison microscope and they may—mind you, I'm telling you they just *may*—be able to prove that the fatal bullet was fired from Edgar's gun without ever having the gun."

Her face showed dismay.

"However," Mason said, "with a small-caliber bullet there's not so much chance of that. Only you say you fired hundreds of shots. What did you use as a target?"

"Edgar had a target. He used to put it in the car. We'd put it up against a bank."

"What kind of a target?"

"He used a dart target," she said. "He had an old target that was made of some kind of a heavy cork, or something of that sort, and used it when he was shooting darts. Then after he quit shooting darts for pleasure, he put a backing of some kind of plywood on this target and then made some paper facings with a compass."

"He was a good shot?"

"A wonderful shot, and he trained me so I became a pretty good shot."

"Always with his gun?"

"Always with his gun. He was sort of a nut on wanting his women to be able to protect themselves. He wanted me to be an expert shot."

"You don't own a gun of your own?"

"No."

"You've never had a gun of your own?"

"No."

"Now, let's be sure about that," Mason said. "You've never made an application to purchase a revolver of any sort. Never had anyone give you a revolver?"

She shook her head in the negative.

Mason was silent for a while.

She said, "I don't think you need to worry too much about that revolver, Mr. Mason. They're never going to find it. Do you want me to tell you what I did with it so you can rest easy and—"

Mason held up his hand. "Keep quiet," he said. "Don't tell me. Don't tell anyone."

"But if I tell you, it's in confidence, isn't it?"

"Some things you can tell me are in confidence," Mason said. "But some things you can tell me would make me an accessory after the fact. I don't want to know where that gun is. I don't want anyone to know where that gun is. I don't want you to ever tell anyone anything about a gun or about being in that apartment. Just keep completely quiet. Say that your attorney doesn't want you to make any statement at this time, that a complete statement will be made sometime later.

"Then if they ask you how much later or anything of that sort you can tell them that it will be up to your attorney to fix the date.

"Where did Edgar keep this target that you mention?"

"I don't know. Somewhere in his garage."

"He had an individual garage?"

"Yes. The apartment house where he had his apart-

ment was one of those where they had individual ga-
rages rather than a central basement garage."

"And his car?" Mason asked.

"That was all smashed up in the automobile accident and was towed away by the police, I believe."

"Did you see the car after the accident?"

"No."

"Did you look in the trunk?"

"No."

"You don't know whether this target might have been
in the trunk?"

"No."

"It could have been?"

"Yes."

Again Mason was thoughtfully silent. Then abruptly
he got to his feet. "All right, Diana," he said, "your
future depends in large part upon keeping quiet and on
an element of luck.

"You have taken it on yourself to disregard just about
every bit of advice I've given you so far, and to try to
substitute your own judgment in place of mine. Now
you're in a jam."

"But I *had* to see Cassel," she said. "Don't you understand, Mr. Mason? You can't afford to take chances
with a blackmailer. You say that you don't pay them
and all that, but you know as well as I do that that's a
high-risk game.

"I didn't want you to fight with this man and take a
chance on doing something that would wreck Edgar's
life. . . . And, of course, at that time I thought Edgar would recover."

"The way you planned it," Mason said, "would have been the high-risk game. You don't get rid of a black-mailer by paying him off. That simply makes him more eager. It postpones the time of the next bite for a few weeks or perhaps a few months, but eventually the blackmailer is always back. He regards his hold on his victim as a certain capital asset, just like owning a gov-ernment bond or having money in the bank."

She shook her head. "I know that's what lawyers al-ways say but you can't be sure. You don't know what he wanted. You don't know what his hold on Edgar was. It may have been something that . . . well, something that I could have protected him on."

"In what way?"

"By paying off, I could have had negatives and prints of pictures and all that."

"Negatives," Mason said, "can be duplicated. Pic-tures can be copied. When you take the word of a black-mailer that you're getting evidence, you're trusting the integrity of the blackmailer and, for the most part, that's a mighty poor risk."

The lawyer pressed a bell button, signaling that the interview was over.

"What's going to happen to me?" she asked.

"That," Mason said, "depends upon many things. But I can tell you one thing, if you start talking, if you try to explain your actions, if you start confiding in the police, you're either going to walk into the gas chamber or spend the better part of your life in the confines of a prison."

"Can't I be released on bail or something?"

Mason shook his head.

A deputy slid open the door. "All finished?" he asked.

"All finished," Mason said. He turned and waved a reassuring hand to Diana Douglas.

Chapter Fourteen

ON HIS return to his office, Mason sent for Paul Drake.

"How does it look?" Della Street asked.

Mason shook his head. "The little fool!"

"What's she done now?"

"Lied to me. Used her judgment in place of mine. Probably left a back trail that the police can follow, but still thinks she's the smart little mastermind that can get away with it."

Drake's knock sounded on the door and Mason nodded to Della.

She opened the door.

"What is it this time?" Drake asked.

"I'm afraid," Mason said, "this is an end to your well-cooked restaurant meals, Paul. I'm afraid you're going back to sitting at the desk during long hours and eating soggy hamburgers which have been sent in from the drive-in on the next corner."

"What now?" Drake asked.

Mason said, "Diana Douglas."

"What's she done now?"

"I don't know," Mason said.

"Well, if you don't, I don't know who would."

Mason said, "I can tell you what the police think she did. The police think she went to the Tallmeyer Apartments on Thursday afternoon, that she went up to the ninth floor, had a conference with Moray Cassel, that Moray Cassel was trying to blackmail her, or perhaps her brother."

"But she paid off?" Drake asked.

"She paid off with a twenty-two-caliber revolver, shooting a particularly powerful brand of twenty-two cartridge."

"And they recovered the bullet?" Drake asked.

"Probably."

"Striations?"

Mason shrugged his shoulders.

"How many times? I mean, how many shots?"

"One, as I understand the facts," Mason said. "The man lived perhaps for some time, but he was unconscious and was unable to move. There was considerable hemorrhage."

"How do they know it's a twenty-two caliber?"

"Well," Mason said, "I'll amend that. They say it's a small caliber. I think probably they mean by that it's a twenty-two caliber. And the police claim that when little Miss Mastermind opened her purse and pulled out the gun she inadvertently jerked her BankAmerica credit card out."

"Which the police have?"

"Which the police have."

"And she claims the shooting was in self defense, or what?"

"She doesn't claim. She's silent."

"Anybody see her go into the apartment?" Drake asked.

"I don't know. She may have left a back trail that can be followed and proven. I'm only telling you what the police claim at the moment. The police claim that her BankAmerica credit card fell out of her purse on the floor without being noticed."

"Fingerprints?" Drake asked.

"I wouldn't know," Mason said.

Drake regarded him shrewdly. "A good possibility they do have fingerprints?"

"Could be."

"And you want me to find out?"

Mason said, "I want you to find out everything you can about the case, Paul. And particularly I want to find out about the victim, Moray Cassel."

"Personal habits, friends, contacts?" Drake asked.

"Everything," Mason said. "Paul, I sized that man up as some sort of a pimp. He's the sort who is making a living out of women or off of women some way and he's trying to disguise the rotten part underneath by a well-groomed exterior.

"Now, I'm particularly anxious to find out about his woman."

"Woman, singular?" Drake asked.

"Well, let's say women, plural," Mason said, "because the guy may have more than one of them. . . .

And, of course, anything you can find out about the police case is something I want to know."

"How soon do you want to know?"

"At once. Relay information just as soon as you can get it."

"Costs?" Drake asked.

Mason said, "I *think* I can get costs out of my client, Paul, but I'm going to share the expense on this one, and if necessary I'll carry the whole load."

Drake raised an inquiring eyebrow.

Mason said, by way of explanation, "This case slipped up on my blind side, Paul. I gave a client the wrong advice right at the start."

"Forget it!" Drake said. "You never made a legal mistake in your life."

"I didn't make a mistake in advising her in regard to the law," Mason said, "but I made a mistake in letting her stick her neck way, way out; and then, notwithstanding the fact that I had been warned about her tendency to disregard a lawyer's advice and do things on her own, I let her out of my sight during the most critical period of all."

"When was that?" Drake asked.

"Confidentially," Mason said, "it was probably the time Moray Cassel was being murdered."

"Okay," Drake said, heaving himself to his feet, "we'll give you the usual trade discount and go to work, Perry."

Chapter Fifteen

JUDGE CHARLES JEROME ELLIOTT looked down from the bench and said, "This is the time fixed for the preliminary hearing in the case of People versus Diana Douglas, charged with the murder of one Moray Cassel. The defendant is in court and is represented by counsel?"

Mason arose. "I am representing the defendant, if the Court please."

Judge Elliott nodded. "And the prosecution?" he asked.

Ralph Gurlock Floyd arose. "I am the trial deputy who will handle the prosecution, Your Honor."

"Very well," Judge Elliott said. "Now, I want to make a statement to both counsel. I am well aware of the fact that in the past counsel for the defense has made spectacular courtroom scenes in connection with preliminary hearings. I don't approve of trying a case at a preliminary hearing.

"The object of a preliminary hearing is to try to find

whether there is a crime which has been committed and if there is reasonable ground to connect the defendant with that crime. In that event the defendant is bound over to the Superior Court for trial before a jury.

"Now then, gentlemen, I am *not* going to test the credibility of witnesses in this Court. I am going to take the evidence at its face value. Once it has been established that a crime has been committed and once evidence has been introduced tending to show the defendant is connected with that crime, this Court is going to make an order binding the defendant over regardless of how much evidence there may be in favor of the defendant.

"In other words, I am not going to try to decide the weight of the evidence or the preponderance of the evidence. Of course, it is understood that in the event the defendant can introduce evidence completely destroying the prosecution's case the situation will be different. But you gentlemen will understand that the chances of that are quite remote.

"Now that we understand the situation, you may go ahead, Mr. Prosecutor; put on your case."

Ralph Gurlock Floyd, a dedicated prosecutor, who had been responsible for more death-penalty verdicts than any prosecutor in the state, and was proud of it, apparently felt that this prosecution of a preliminary hearing was somewhat beneath his dignity. But, having been assigned by Hamilton Burger, the District Attorney, to prosecute the case, he went about it with the savage, vindictiveness which was so characteristic of his courtroom manner.

His first witness was a chambermaid at the Tallmeyer Apartments.

"Did you," he asked, "know Moray Cassel in his lifetime?"

"I did."

"When did you last see him alive?"

"On Tuesday, the tenth of this month."

"At what time?"

"At about four o'clock in the afternoon."

"When did you next see him?"

"On the evening of Sunday, the fifteenth."

"Was he alive?"

"He was dead."

"What did you do?"

"I notified the manager of the apartment house, who notified the police."

"Cross-examine," Floyd snapped.

"No questions," Mason said.

A police officer was called as a witness, then a deputy coroner. A diagram was introduced showing the position of the body on the bed as of 9 P.M. on Sunday, the fifteenth, when the body was discovered and the position of the various articles of furniture in the apartment.

Floyd next called William Ardley, the police officer who testified to searching the apartment for significant clues.

"What did you find?"

"I found a BankAmerica credit card issued to one Diana Douglas of San Francisco."

"What did you do with that card?"

"I marked it for identification by punching two small holes in it in certain places which I selected."

"I show you what purports to be a credit card from the Bank of America and ask you if you have seen that before."

"That is the identical credit card."

"You're positive?"

"The card is the same and the pin holes are in the exact location that I placed them."

"Cross-examine," Floyd said.

"No questions," Mason announced cheerfully.

Floyd regarded him thoughtfully, then put a finger-print technician on the stand who testified to finding quite a few latent fingerprints in the apartment. Some of them were the fingerprints of the decedent. Some of them were the fingerprints of the maid who cleaned the apartment twice a week.

"Any other fingerprints?" Floyd asked.

"There were some we couldn't identify."

"Any others that you could?"

"Yes, sir. Two of them."

"Where were they?"

"One of them was in the bathroom on the mirror of the medicine chest. The other one was on a nightstand table by the side of the bed where the body was lying."

"Did you determine the identity of these finger-prints?"

"We did, yes, sir. One of them is the middle finger of the defendant's right hand. The other is the thumb of the defendant's right hand."

"You're positive?"

"We have more than enough points of similarity and several unusual characteristics."

"Anything else in the bathroom?"

"There was a towel with blood stains on it, a moist towel where someone had evidently washed—"

"Objected to as conclusion of the witness," Mason said.

"Sustained," Judge Elliott snapped.

"A bloody towel," the witness said.

"You have that here?"

"Yes, sir."

"Produce it, please."

The witness produced a sealed paper bag, opened it, and took out a hand towel with the words TALL-MEYER APARTMENTS embroidered in the corner. The towel was stained a faint rusty color.

"We offer to introduce it in evidence as People's Exhibit B," Floyd said.

"No objection," Mason observed casually.

"You photographed the latent fingerprints?" Floyd asked.

"I did."

"Will you produce those photographs, please?"

The photographs of the latent prints were produced and introduced in evidence. The prosecutor then introduced a whole series of photographs, showing the decedent on the bed with blood which had saturated the pillow, dripped down to the floor, and spread over the carpet.

An autopsy surgeon was called as a witness. He testified that he had recovered the fatal bullet from the back of the skull; that the bullet was of a type known as a .22-caliber, long rifle bullet; that it had penetrated the forehead on the median line about two inches above the eyes; that there had been a very considerable hemorrhage.

"When did death occur?" the prosecutor asked.

"In my opinion, making all of the tests we could, death occurred sometime between two o'clock on the afternoon of Thursday, the twelfth and five o'clock in the morning on Saturday, the fourteenth."

"Was death instantaneous?"

"No, I don't think so. Unconsciousness immediately followed the shot, and there was probably no movement of the body. But, despite the fact the victim was unconscious, the heart continued to pump blood into the brain which accounted for the very extensive hemorrhage. Death may have resulted in a period of ten or fifteen minutes after the fatal shot, or it may have been an hour. I can't tell."

"You say you recovered the fatal bullet?"

"Yes, sir."

"What did you do with it?"

"I delivered it to the ballistics expert in the presence of two witnesses."

"Could you determine the weapon from which that bullet had been fired?"

"Not definitely at the moment. We knew that it must have been fired from one of several makes of guns and we rather suspected that it had been fired from a gun with a long barrel because of—"

"Move to strike out what the witness rather suspected," Mason said.

"It will go out," Judge Elliott ruled. "Stick to facts, Mr. Witness."

"Very well," Floyd said with a triumphant smile. "We'll withdraw this witness for the moment and put on other witnesses, then recall him. I will call Miss Smith, please."

Miss Smith turned out to be a neatly dressed young woman in her early thirties.

"What is your occupation?"

"I am employed at the ticket counter of United Airlines at the Los Angeles Terminal."

"Were you so employed on Thursday, the twelfth of this month?"

"I was."

"I will ask you to look at the defendant and tell us if you have ever seen her before."

"Yes, sir, I have."

"Where?"

"At the ticket counter on the evening of Thursday, the twelfth."

"At about what time?"

"It was exactly six-forty P.M."

"Did you have a conversation with her?"

"Yes."

"And what was that conversation?"

"She was very anxious to know if the plane which was due to leave at six twenty-seven had left on time or whether it would be possible for her to get aboard. I told her that the plane had left only about five minutes late, that she would have to wait approximately an hour and twenty minutes and take a flight leaving at eight o'clock."

"What did she do?"

"She asked for a ticket to San Francisco."

"And then?" Floyd asked, his manner triumphant.

"Then she produced her purse and said, 'I'll pay for it with a BankAmerica credit card.' Then she raised her purse so I could briefly see it and suddenly dropped it down out of sight."

"You say, suddenly?"

"Suddenly and self-consciously."

"Was there any reason for such action?"

"She had a gun in her purse."

"What sort of a gun?"

"A long-barreled gun with a wooden handle."

"When you say a gun, you mean a revolver?"

"Yes, sir."

"Then what happened?"

"Then she fumbled around in her purse, keeping it below the counter so I couldn't see inside of it, and said, 'Oh, I seem to have misplaced my BankAmericard.' Then she thought for a moment and said, 'Did Mr. Perry Mason, the lawyer, leave a ticket here for me?'

"I told her that Mr. Mason had left two tickets which had been charged to his air-travel card. One ticket he had picked up, and the other one he had left to be picked up by Diana Douglas.

"Her face showed relief and she said, 'I am Diana Douglas. I'll take the ticket, please.' "

"So you gave her the ticket?"

"Yes."

"And then what?"

"Then she left and I made it a point to look at the purse she was carrying. The gun in it distorted the purse's shape and—"

"Move to strike out that it was the gun that had distorted the purse's shape," Mason said.

Judge Elliott hesitated, then said, "That may go out. The witness can state whether the purse was distorted."

"The purse was distorted by some object which had been thrust into the purse, an object so long that the purse was out of shape."

"Cross-examine," Floyd said.

"Did you," Mason asked, "ever pick the defendant out of a line-up?"

"No, I didn't."

"You didn't see her from the time you talked with her at the ticket counter until you went into the courtroom today?"

"I identified her picture."

"But you didn't pick her out of a line-up?"

"I did not. That wasn't at all necessary, Mr. Mason. After the manner in which my attention had been attracted to the defendant, I would have picked her out anywhere."

"That's all," Mason said.

Floyd put on his next witness with an air of triumph. He was a middle-aged individual who gave his occupation as part of a crew who cleaned up airplanes for the United Airlines.

"Are you familiar with the plane which left the Los Angeles Airport Terminal at eight o'clock on the evening of Thursday, the twelfth of this month, and arrived in San Francisco approximately an hour later?"

"Yes, sir."

"Did you clean that plane?"

"Yes, sir."

"Did you find anything unusual?"

"I did."

"What was it?"

"It was a gun."

"Where was that gun found?"

"The gun had been concealed in an opening underneath a pile of towels in one of the lavatories. I may state that these towels are placed in piles in the containers and are replenished from time to time. On this particular occasion I wanted to get at one of the connections for the plumbing, and in order to do that I had to remove the towels and insert my hand in the opening in the back of the towels. When I did that I felt some foreign object in there and drew it out, and it was this gun."

"Did you take any steps to identify the gun?"

"I took it to my supervisor."

"And what did the supervisor do?"

"He notified the police and, at the request of the police, we took down the statistics on the weapon."

"What were the statistics?"

"This was a twenty-two caliber single-action revolver, having a nine-and-three-eighth-inch barrel and a wooden handle. On the gun was stamped Ruger twenty-two, with the words single six, the number, one-three-nine-five-seven-three and the name of the manufacturer, Sturm—S-T-U-R-M—Ruger—R-U-G-E-R—and Company, Southport, Connecticut. The initials E.D. had been carved in the handle."

"I'll show you a gun and ask you if that is the gun that you found."

Floyd came forward and handed the witness the gun.

Diana Douglas' hand clutched Mason's leg, the fingers digging in so hard that the lawyer surreptitiously lowered his own hand to loosen her grip.

Diana's face was tense, tight-lipped and chalky.

The witness turned the gun over in his fingers, nodded, and said, "This is the gun."

"What was the condition of the gun when you found it?"

"It was fully loaded except for one shell which had been discharged."

"This is a single-action gun, and, in other words, it has to be cocked and then the trigger pulled. It isn't the so-called self-cocking gun?"

"No, sir, it is what is known as a single-action gun."

"Cross-examine," Floyd said.

"You have no idea how long the gun had been in that receptacle?" Mason asked.

"No, sir. I know when I found it, that's all."

"Thank you," Mason said, "no further questions."

Floyd introduced in evidence the sales register of the Sacramento Sporting Dealers, Inc., showing that the

Ruger gun in question had been sold five years earlier to Edgar Douglas.

His next witness was a young woman who identified herself as a hostess on the eight o'clock plane to San Francisco on the night of Thursday, the twelfth. She had noticed Diana, observed that she was a passenger, had observed the peculiar shape of the cloth purse she was carrying when she boarded the plane. She stated that Diana was carrying a sort of overnight bag as well as the cloth purse, and when Diana went to the lavatory she noticed that she carried both the overnight bag and the purse with her, which the stewardess thought was rather peculiar. Aside from that, however, she could contribute no evidence. She hadn't paid any particular attention to the purse after Diana had been in the lavatory.

Then Floyd pulled his trump witness, the ballistics expert who stated that the fatal bullet which had killed Moray Cassel had come from the gun which had been registered in the name of Edgar Douglas.

This expert was followed by the manager of the San Francisco apartment house, who stated that after the automobile accident which had rendered Edgar Douglas unconscious and had resulted in his going to the hospital, his sister, the defendant, had been given a key to her brother's apartment and had been in and out, straightening things up.

Next Floyd introduced the doorman at the Tall-meyer Apartments. He had, he admitted, not seen the defendant when she entered the apartments, but he had

seen her when she left; he noticed she had been carrying a black type of overnight bag and a black cloth
purse. The purse was stretched to the limit by some
rigid object which was within it. He had noticed the
purse particularly.

Floyd introduced a purse which was identified as the
property of the defendant and asked the doorman if he
recognized the purse. The doorman answered in the
affirmative. It was either that purse or one that was an
exact duplicate of it.

Judge Elliott glanced at the clock and cleared his
throat. "Gentlemen, it is nearing the hour of adjourn-
ment and it would certainly seem there is no use in
prolonging this inquiry further. There is undoubtedly
evidence that a crime has been committed and an abun-
dance of evidence connecting the defendant with the
crime. In fact, the Court has been rather surprised at
the amount of detailed evidence put on by the prosecution."

Floyd said, "The prosecution is all too well aware of
the reputation of defense counsel and wishes to leave
no possible loophole."

"Well, it would seem that you have left no loophole,"
Judge Elliott said, smiling. "I think, gentlemen, we
can adjourn the hearing and bind the defendant over."

Mason arose. "If the Court please," he said with re-
spect but very firmly, "the defense may wish to put on
some testimony."

"Why?" Judge Elliott asked.

"Because I believe it is our right."

"You have a right to subpoena witnesses, that is true.

But this Court is not called upon to judge the credibility of witnesses. This Court is not called upon to weigh questions of reasonable doubt. You certainly can't claim that a *prima facie* case has not been established."

"The question of whether a *prima facie* case has been established," Mason said, "depends upon the evidence at the conclusion of the case and any attempt to decide a case without giving the defendant a day in court would be—"

"Oh, all right, all right," Judge Elliott said impatiently. "We'll continue the case until ten o'clock tomorrow morning. I want to warn counsel, however, that we have a busy calendar and the Court does not take kindly to fishing expeditions or attempts to try a case on the merits at a preliminary hearing. The Court warns counsel that this Court will not weigh the credibility of witnesses and that any question of conflicting facts will be determined in favor of the prosecution as far as this hearing is concerned. However, the Court will try to do nothing which will preclude the defendant from having a fair hearing on the merits before a jury in the Superior Court, at which time the credibility of witnesses can be raised and the doctrine of reasonable doubt will apply.

"It is simply a case of differing procedures in different courts. Do you understand that, Mr. Mason?"

"I understand it," Mason said.

"Very well. The case is adjourned until ten o'clock tomorrow morning."

Mason placed a reassuring hand on Diana's shoulder. "Keep a stiff upper lip, Diana," he said.

"They're going to bind me over to the Superior Court?"

"Probably," Mason said, "but I want to find out as much about the case as I can before the Court makes its order."

"And what happens when I get to the Superior Court?"

"You are tried by a jury. You have the benefit of any reasonable doubt."

Mason bent forward to say in a low voice, "Where did you get that gun?"

"Just as I told you, Mr. Mason. It was on the floor with blood on it. I took it in the bathroom and washed the blood off and then put the gun in my purse. I had a hard time getting it in, and I guess that's when I lost the credit card."

"And you hid it in the airplane?"

"Yes, I took out the towels and felt all around in the back of the towel compartment and found this little opening way in back. I thought they'd never find the gun in there."

Mason said, "Tell me—about the girls in the San Francisco office. Do you know who could have written that message to me?"

"It might have been any one of them."

"It was written on an electric typewriter."

"All the typewriters are electric," she said.

"All right," Mason told her, "keep a stiff upper lip. I'll see you in the morning."

The lawyer picked up his briefcase and left the courtroom.

Chapter Sixteen

PERRY MASON, Della Street, and Paul Drake were huddled around a table in an Italian restaurant which was near the courthouse and where the proprietor was accustomed to devoting a small private dining room to the exclusive use of the trio.

"Well," Drake said, "it looks as if the judge has his mind made up, from all I could hear."

Mason nodded. "What have you found out, Paul?"

"Not a whole lot," Drake admitted, "a lot of detached bits of information. I don't know whether they'll do you any good. . . . As you, yourself, have remarked, your client is an awful liar."

"She is and she isn't," Mason said. "She lied to me because she wanted to save her brother's reputation. She thought there was something that was hanging over his head, something that he'd pay five thousand dollars to eliminate. She wanted to carry out his wishes.

"Therefore, she acted independently of my advice and she tried to deceive me, but when it came to a showdown I don't think she did try to deceive me. At least, I think there's a possibility she's telling the truth.

"That's a duty that a lawyer owes to his client. Regardless of how many times he has been lied to in the past, he always has to keep the faith. He always has to believe that in the final showdown, the client is telling the truth and putting the cards face up on the table."

Drake said, "She can't be telling the truth on this one, Perry. She went down there and tried to buy him off. She couldn't do it and she killed him."

"What have you found out?" Mason asked, detouring the subject.

"Well," Drake said, "you probably had Moray Cassel pretty well pegged. The guy lived a mysterious life, and no one knows his real source of income or how much his income was.

"This much I did find out. The man was always armed. He carried a thirty-eight-caliber, snub-nosed revolver in a shoulder holster under his left armpit. His clothes were tailor-made, and for years the same tailor had been making his clothes and making them so that there was an extra bit of room under the left armpit so the bulge made by the gun wouldn't be conspicuous."

"The deuce!" Mason said.

Drake nodded.

"And that gun was on him at the time his body was found?"

"It must have been," Drake said.

Mason's eyes narrowed. "Now, isn't it interesting that the police described everything in the room, showed photographs of the body lying fully clothed on the bed with a bullet hole in the forehead, the blood all over the pillow and down on the floor, and no one said anything about the gun?"

"Did you ask them?" Drake inquired.

Mason grinned. "I didn't ask them. I wouldn't have thought to have asked them about a gun, but I certainly should have thought to have asked them what was found in his pockets and whether anything significant was found in the room. . . . What about the source of income, Paul?"

Drake shook his head. "The guy did everything with cash. He wore a money belt. There were four one-thousand-dollar bills in the money belt. He had a leather wallet that was pretty well crammed with hundred-dollar bills. As nearly as can be found out he had no bank account. He bought that Cadillac automobile and paid for it with cold, hard cash."

"Women?" Mason asked.

"Women came to see him from time to time."

"The same woman or different women?"

"Different."

"What did you find out about the note that was placed on the display case in San Francisco where I'd pick it up?"

"The note was written on an electric typewriter," Drake said. "They're all electric typewriters, but this particular note, as nearly as I can determine, was written on the typewriter of Joyce Baffin.

"For your information, Perry, if it's worth anything, Joyce Baffin left the import-export office at noon, Thursday, pleading a terrific headache. She was, however, back on the job Friday morning, and Joyce was and is very popular with the officials and employees of the company and was at one time very friendly with Edgar Douglas. In fact, he had quite a crush on her. But so did lots of other people. Perhaps Franklin Gage, who is a widower, and Homer Gage, who has a predatory eye, would have liked to enjoy a closer relationship with Joyce Baffin."

Mason, sipping a cocktail, digested that information.

Drake went on. "I have some more odds and ends of various bits of information. I spent quite a bit of time and a fair amount of money with the telephone operator at Tallmeyer Apartments. I found out that Moray Cassel put through a lot of telephone calls to a local number. I found that number was the apartment of one Irene Blodgett, twenty-seven, blond, Millsep Apartments, divorced, employed steadily during the daytime at the Underwood Importing Company. At night she's something of a gadabout but never anything spectacular. Quiet, refined, good-looking, popular—I've got operatives working quietly on her, but if there's anything phony she's pretty well covered.

"The only thing is that this Underwood Importing Company does have some dealing or has had dealings with the Escobar Import and Export Company."

Della Street, watching Mason's face, said, "You have an idea, Chief?"

"Just this," Mason said. "At the time of his death, Moray Cassel was either standing by the bed or sitting on the edge of the bed. He was shot in the forehead by one shot from a high-powered, single-action, twenty-two-caliber revolver with a nine-and-three-eighth-inch barrel. The murderer must have been facing him."

"Well?" Drake asked. "What's so peculiar about that? Diana Douglas went to call on the guy. She rang the bell. Cassel let her in. She tried to bargain with him, then he got tough with her. She knew at that time that blackmailers never quit. Once they get a hold on a victim they bleed him white. Diana was obsessed with the idea she had to protect her brother."

Mason held the stem of his cocktail glass, watching the liquid on the inside as he twisted the glass between his thumb and forefinger.

"You got into Cassel's apartment?" he asked the detective.

"Sure, after the police were through with it. That seemed to take an awful long while. They went over the whole place dusting for fingerprints, testing for blood stains, and all that."

"What about the fellow's wardrobe?" Mason asked. "Was he meticulous with his clothes as I thought?"

"Boy, you've said it," Drake replied. "It was a fairly large-sized apartment with lots of drawer space. The drawers were filled with monogrammed shirts. He even had monograms on his underwear, and the closet was pretty well filled with tailor-made clothes."

"You checked with his tailor?"

"Sure. The tailor told me that Cassel always paid him in cash, seldom wore a suit over six months, and was very fastidious. And, of course, there was that bit about tailoring the suits so the bulge didn't show where the revolver was carried under the left armpit.

"The tailor got quite friendly with me, said that he always had an idea Cassel was a gangster of some sort, and was very certain that Cassel was cheating on the income tax. But, of course, it was none of the tailor's business, and, believe me, the tailor loved to get that money in the form of cash. . . . I wouldn't be too surprised, Perry, if perhaps the tailor didn't do a little cheating on the income tax himself."

"What about overcoats?" Mason asked. "Were those tailor-made, too?"

"Everything," Drake said. "Now, wait a minute, Perry, there's one exception. There was one overcoat in there that Cassel had evidently used for rough-and-tumble stuff when he was loading or unloading things in an automobile."

"What makes you say that?"

"Well, it was an overcoat that wasn't tailor-made and the labels had been cut out from both the neck and the breast pocket."

"The deuce you say," Mason said. And then, after a while, "How did it fit, Paul?"

"How should I know?" Drake asked. "The corpse was being dissected in the medical examiner's office at the coroner's by an autopsy surgeon. I couldn't very well go in there and try on an overcoat. . . . He couldn't have had it on since late spring. It had been hot for the whole week of the murder. . . . What difference does the one coat make?"

Mason sat for a long moment in contemplative silence, then abruptly changed the subject. "You have the various telephone numbers of the personnel at the Escobar Import and Export Company?"

Drake nodded.

Mason said to Della Street, "See if you can get us a telephone, Della."

When a telephone had been brought into the room and connected, Mason used his credit card, saying, "This is a credit-card call. I want to talk with Franklin Gage at this number in San Francisco."

Mason took Drake's notebook and read the number of Franklin Gage's residence.

"It's a person-to-person call. No one else if he's out."

The lawyer drummed with the fingers of his right hand while he held the telephone to his ear. "Let's hope we're in luck," he said.

A moment later he heard the suave voice of Franklin Gage on the telephone.

"This is Perry Mason, the lawyer," Mason said. "I take it that you are somewhat interested in this case against Diana Douglas, who is working for you . . . for your company, that is."

"Well, in a way," Gage said cautiously. "It depends upon what you want."

"Has an audit been completed of the cash shortage of your import company?"

"Yes, it has."

"Would you mind telling me what it shows?"

"In round figures," Gage said, "it shows a shortage of ten thousand dollars."

Mason said, "Would you be willing to do something which might prevent a miscarriage of justice, Mr. Gage?"

"What?"

"I would like to see that Joyce Baffin is present in court tomorrow morning when the case against Diana Douglas is called up."

"Well, of course, if you want to pay her expenses down and back," Gage said, "I would give her a leave of absence."

"It's not that," Mason said. "She might not want to come."

"Well, I certainly can't force her to come."

Mason said, "She has been in your employ for some time?"

"Yes, all of the secretaries have been with us for quite some time. We don't have a turnover with help, Mr. Mason. Our business is highly specialized, and after we have trained a young woman to perform competent secretarial duties we try to keep her."

Mason said, "The reason I am calling you personally, Mr. Gage, is that it is tremendously important that Joyce Baffin be here. I can't begin to tell you how vital it may be. I am going to ask that you and your nephew, Homer Gage, come down to Los Angeles to the trial, that you personally get in touch with Joyce Baffin tonight and tell her that it is highly important that the three of you come down."

"The *three* of us!" Gage echoed.

"Exactly," Mason said. "I have reason to believe that if you ask her to come down by herself she might not come. She might even skip out. And, if only one of you is coming with her, she might again become suspicious. But if both you and your nephew are coming down ostensibly to see what you can do to help Diana Douglas—"

"If she's guilty, she's not entitled to any help," Gage interrupted sternly.

"But suppose she isn't guilty? You've had a chance to study the young woman. You've had a chance to know something of her loyalty. Do you think that she's the type of a woman who would commit a murder?"

"Well, of course," Gage said cautiously, "you never know what a person will do when they're hard pressed, and she always tried to protect her brother, but— Do you feel this is really important, Mr. Mason?"

"I feel that it is highly important. I feel that it is vital," Mason said.

There was silence at the other end of the line.

"If you can do exactly as I suggested," Mason said, "I feel that it will be possible to eliminate certain questions which might otherwise come up in court."

"What sort of questions?"

"Oh, about the Escobar Import and Export Company, the nature of its business, the large amount of cash that it keeps on hand, and all of those things that are business details which you *might* not care to have your competitors know about."

"Very well," Gage said quickly, "if I can have your assurance that you feel this will keep the business affairs of our company out of evidence, Mr. Mason, and if you assure me that it is vital to the case of your client,

Homer and I will do our best to induce Joyce to come
with us, and I feel that we can be successful. . . .
Where and when do we meet you?"

"You take a plane tonight," Mason said, "so you will
be sure to get in. You go to a hotel. All you have to do is
to ring up the Drake Detective Agency and Paul Drake
will send a car to escort you to the courtroom tomorrow morning, see that you are given admission, and
properly seated."

"The Drake Detective Agency," Gage said.

"That's right," Mason said, and gave him Paul
Drake's number.

"Very well. We'll do it."

"I can depend on you?" Mason asked.

"You have my word," Franklin Gage said with dignity.

"That's good enough for me," Mason told him, and
hung up the telephone.

"Now, what the hell?" Drake asked.

Mason picked up the cocktail glass, drained it, and
smiled. "I think," he said, "I'm beginning to see day-
light. . . . A shortage of *ten* thousand dollars."

"The original figure was twenty thousand," Drake
said.

Mason nodded. "Remember, however, that when
Franklin Gage entered the office he said that he had
been working on a business deal and had taken ten
thousand dollars out, that the deal had fallen through
and he was in the process of replacing the ten thousand
dollars in the cash drawer."

"I don't get it," Drake said.

"If we can get those people in court tomorrow morning perhaps we'll get lucky," Mason said.

"But you assured them that those business matters wouldn't come out."

"I think they won't," Mason told him. "Now then, I'm going to have another cocktail and then we're going to order one of these fabulous Italian dinners and relax while we eat it."

Chapter Seventeen

RALPH GURLOCK FLOYD arose with something of a
flourish when the case of the People vs. Diana Douglas
was called.

"I think, if the Court please, we can rest the prosecution's case."

"I certainly would think so," Judge Elliott said. "In
fact, I think this whole matter could have been disposed
of yesterday afternoon. I take it there is no defense."

"Indeed there is a defense," Mason said.

"I want to repeat that this court is not interested in
fishing expeditions, Mr. Mason. I am not going to preclude the defendant from putting on any legitimate defense, but it would seem virtually mathematical that
there is no defense and can be no defense to the array
of facts which have been marshaled this far by witnesses."

"If the Court please," Mason said, "I would like to
recall one of the officers for just one or two questions on
further cross-examination."

"That's irregular," Floyd protested. "That motion should have been made earlier."

"Oh, come, come," Judge Elliott said, "one thing is certain. I'm not going to preclude this defendant from an opportunity to cross-examine any witness of the prosecution. I take it, Mr. Mason, there's some particular significance in connection with this?"

"There is, Your Honor."

"Recall the witness," Judge Elliott said.

Mason motioned to the officer. "Take the stand," he said. "Remember you've already been sworn. Now, you have the bag which has been identified as the cloth purse which the defendant had in her possession when the ticket seller at the airlines saw the gun in the purse, the same purse which the stewardess noticed on the airplane?"

"That's right."

"You have both the gun and the purse," Mason said. "Now, have you tried putting the gun in the purse?"

The officer smiled patronizingly. "Of course we have. It fits so snugly that the cloth is stretched tight and the purse is bulged out of shape. That's why it was so noticeable."

"Please put the gun in the purse," Mason said.

The clerk handed the two exhibits to the officer. He took the purse, opened it, inserted the muzzle of the gun, then gradually worked the gun into the purse, explaining as he did so, "You can see what a snug fit it is and how it is necessary to twist the cloth of the purse so it fits over the grip of the gun, which, of course," he added with a quick look of triumph at the Deputy District Attorney, "explains why the defendant lost the credit card out of the purse when she was taking the gun out."

"All right," Mason said, "you have the gun in the purse now."

"That's right."

"And you can close the purse?"

"Yes, you can barely close the purse, and," the witness went on, "when you open the purse anyone who looks in it can see a part of the gun . . . the wooden butt of the weapon."

"Exactly," Mason said. "Now, a gun has two outlines, the convex outline and a concave outline, does it not?"

"I don't understand what you mean," the officer said.

"Well," Mason said, "a gun is made generally on a curve so that when you hold the butt of the gun in your hand in a shooting position the barrel of the gun is elevated so that you can aim down it."

"Oh, certainly, that's right."

"And, by the same sign, when you turn the gun over, the position is reversed. That is what I would call the concave position."

"All right," the officer said.

"Now then," Mason said, "you have put the gun in the purse in a concave position. Could you reverse that position and put it in a convex position?"

"Not and close the purse," the officer said. "The fit is too snug. In fact, I don't know if you could even get the gun in the purse in what you refer to as the convex position."

"All right," Mason said, "now, it's taken you a little time to get the gun in the purse."

"It's a snug fit," the officer admitted.

"Now, take it out," Mason said. "Let's see how fast you can take it out."

"What do you mean, how fast I can take it out?"

Mason turned up his wrist and consulted the second hand of his wristwatch. "Let's see exactly how long it takes you to take the gun out."

"Oh, I see," the officer said, "one of those tests, uh?"

He started pulling frantically at the gun in the purse, managed only to jam it tighter against the cloth. To get the gun out, it was necessary for him to take the top of the purse and start pulling the cloth back a fold at a time.

"Five seconds," Mason said.

The officer fumbled frantically.

"Ten seconds," Mason said. "Twelve seconds. Now, you have the gun out. Now, it is in an upside-down position. If you wanted to shoot it you'd have to turn it around in your hand. Please do so."

The officer shifted the gun rapidly in his hand.

"Now, that is a single-action gun," Mason went on. "It can't be cocked and discharged by simply pulling the trigger. You have to pull back the hammer. Do that."

The officer did so.

Mason smiled. "Do you think you could beat that time?"

"Oh, sure, I could," the officer said, "now that I know what you're getting at I could beat it all to pieces."

"All right," Mason said, "put the gun back in the purse, close the purse; then get ready, pull the gun out of the purse, turn it to a firing position, cock the hammer of the gun, and pull the trigger. Start when I say 'ready', and we'll time it until the trigger clicks."

"I'm afraid I don't see the object of this test, interesting as it may be," Judge Elliott said.

"It is simply this, Your Honor," Mason said. "Moray Cassel, the victim, was shot in the forehead by one bullet. Moray Cassel was wearing a revolver in a shoulder holster at the time of his death. I understand that he habitually carried this weapon with him.

"Is it reasonable to suppose that he stood there inactive while the defendant fumbled with her purse and—"

"I see, I see," Judge Elliott said. "Go ahead with the test."

Ralph Gurlock Floyd was on his feet. "We object, Your Honor. It's not a fair test. It is not conducted in accordance with conditions as they existed at the time of the crime. How do we know that the defendant had the gun in what Mr. Mason calls a concave position in her purse when she entered Cassel's apartment. She might have stood outside of the door and done all of the fumbling before Cassel opened the door.

"In that event she would have had the gun in her hand, ready to fire."

"Nevertheless," Judge Elliott said, frowning thoughtfully, "it's an interesting hypothesis and the Court is not going to preclude the defendant the opportunity to advance it. Go ahead, let's make the test and take the time."

This time the officer, knowing what was required and working frantically, was able to cut the time down to approximately seven seconds.

Judge Elliott, who had been watching the performance, said, "The Court gets it at about six seconds."

"Between six and seven seconds," Mason said, "to the time of the click. However, that's good enough."

"Your Honor," Floyd protested, "this is absolutely meaningless. The defendant could have had the gun out of the purse, cocked and ready to shoot before pressing the buzzer so that Moray Cassel would have opened the door to find himself helpless."

"And what happened then?" Mason asked Floyd.

"Don't try to cross-examine me," Floyd snapped.

Mason said with a smile, "I will address my remarks to the Court. The idea of having the defendant ring the buzzer with a gun, loaded and cocked and ready to shoot, would necessitate that the decedent be shot while he was at the door. In place of that the decedent was shot at the far end of the apartment, either while he was standing by the bed or sitting on the bed, and he was shot from some distance since there is no powder tattoo around the edges of the wound."

"We'll argue the case at the proper time," Judge Elliott said. "You have made your point, Mr. Mason."

Floyd said, "The defendant could have had the drop on him and forced him back a step at a time."

"For what purpose?" Mason asked.

"In order to intimidate him," Floyd said. "Who else would have had her brother's gun and— Oh, this is absurd, too absurd to even waste time on."

"Then why are you wasting it?" Mason asked.

"Don't try to question me," Floyd shouted irritably.

"I beg the Court's pardon," Mason said. "I was merely retorting to a retort."

Judge Elliott smiled. "Proceed with your case, Mr. Mason. Do you have any questions of this witness on further cross-examination?"

"I have one or two more questions of this witness, if the Court please," Mason said.

He turned to the officer. "You made a careful examination of the apartment?"

"I did. Several of us did."

"And you noticed the wardrobe of the decedent?"

The officer smiled. "I certainly did."

"It was rather elaborate?"

"That's an understatement. It was *very* elaborate."

"And did you notice that the clothes were tailor-made?"

"The outer garments, yes sir. The under garments were also, I think, custom-made, at least they were initialed."

"And in that collection of outer garments would you say that *all* of them were tailor-made?"

"Yes, sir, all of them."

"*All* of them?"

"All— Now, wait a minute. There was one overcoat in there that didn't have a tailor's label."

"And did you notice that overcoat, try it for size to see whether or not it would have fit the decedent?"

"Well," the officer said, "we didn't try it on the decedent, if that's what you mean."

"How long," Mason asked, "would it take to have this coat brought into court?"

"Oh, Your Honor," Ralph Floyd said in the tone of voice of one whose patience has been taxed to the limit, "this is absurd, this approaches the ridiculous. *I* don't know where this coat is. I suppose it's somewhere in the coroner's office. . . . The Court has said that it wouldn't encourage fishing expeditions and if this isn't a fishing expedition I don't know one when I see it."

Judge Elliott started to nod his head, then frowned thoughtfully and glanced at Mason. "Do you care to make a statement, Mr. Mason?"

"I care to make a statement," Mason said. "I would like to have that coat brought into court. I think it is a vital clue in this case. I have one more question to ask of this witness and then I am finished with my cross-examination. I will start to put on the defendant's case. The first witness will be Stella Grimes, a private detective. Before her testimony is finished, I think that coat should be in court. I also have subpoenaed the tailor who made all of Moray Cassel's clothes, who will testify that this overcoat was not made by him and would not have fit Moray Cassel."

"Go ahead, finish your cross-examination of this witness," Judge Elliott said, "and the Court will direct the prosecution to take steps to have the coat in question brought into court. . . . If this is a fishing expedition it is certainly using most unusual bait.

"Go ahead, Mr. Mason."

Mason said, "You were present in the laboratory when the gun which was recovered from the airplane was tested and examined?"

"Yes."

"For fingerprints?"

"Yes."

"Were there any fingerprints you could find?"

"Nothing that was identifiable. You must understand, Mr. Mason, that regardless of popular fiction stories, the finding of a fingerprint upon a gun—that is, an identifiable latent fingerprint—is not only the exception but it only happens once in a very great number of cases."

"I understand," Mason said. "Now, there are other tests to which that gun was subjected."

"You mean the ballistic tests?"

"No, I meant tests for blood."

The witness hesitated, then said, "Yes, there were tests for blood. There are very sensitive tests which show up blood even when the blood can't be classified."

"The benzidine test?" Mason asked.

"That is one."

"Was a benzidine test performed upon this gun?"

"It was."

"With what result?"

The witness hesitated, then chose his words carefully. "There were widespread reactions. Evidently the gun had been exposed to blood over almost its entire surface. More probably it had been exposed to a concentration of blood and then someone had attempted to wash that blood off very hastily with water or with a damp rag."

"That concludes my cross-examination," Mason said.

"Any redirect?" Judge Elliott asked Ralph Floyd.

"Certainly not," Ralph Floyd said. "We consider these so-called points completely extraneous."

"Now, you have a case to put on for the defense, Mr. Mason?"

"Yes, I will call my first witness, Miss Stella Grimes."

Stella Grimes came forward, gave her name, age, occupation, and residence.

"When did you first see the defendant in this case?" Mason asked.

"It was at night. Mr. Drake and I were in a taxicab. We both wore dark glasses. Mr. Drake had put an ad in the paper suggesting that the person who had money to pay could make the payment to a person in a taxicab at a certain place."

"Did you talk to the defendant at that time?"

"No, she walked past two or three times, but gave no sign of recognition, no indication that she wished to convey any message."

"When did you next see her?"

"The following day."

"Where?"

"At the Willatson Hotel."

"What room?"

"Room Seven-sixty-seven."

"And what happened while you were there?"

"I was instructed to take over as the occupant of that room."

"And the real occupant of that room was the defendant?"

"That's right."

"And what was done with her?"

"You had rented another room down the hall. You took the defendant down to that room."

"Then what happened?"

"Then there was a knock at the door and the decedent paid us a visit."

"By the decedent, you mean Moray Cassel?"

"Yes, sir."

"And what was the conversation?"

"It was very apparent that he was expecting a payment of money, that he expected this from a man, that when he saw that two people were in the room he became suspicious and thought that perhaps a trap was being laid for him."

"So, what did you do?"

"I followed a code signal from you, Mr. Mason. I pretended that I was simply a girl friend who was paying you a visit for purposes of affection. I gave you a casual kiss, departed, but, in accordance with your code signal, I rented a taxicab, watched the exit of the hotel so that I could follow Mr. Cassel when he left, and did so follow him to the Tallmeyer Apartments.

"I then reported to you, giving you the license number of the Cadillac owned by the decedent and the address to which he had driven."

"And then?" Mason asked.

"Then I returned, and continued to occupy the room, waiting for someone to get in touch with me seeking a blackmail payment."

"When the defendant was in the room did you see her purse?"

"I did."

"The purse which has been introduced in evidence and which I now hand you?"

"It was either this purse or a similar one."

Mason said, "I now put the gun which is supposed to have fired the fatal bullet into this purse and ask you if, in your opinion, that gun could have been in that purse at the time that the defendant left the room."

"It definitely could not have been in the purse, not that gun. I would have noticed the manner in which the purse was bulged out of shape."

"Cross-examine," Mason said to Ralph Floyd.

Floyd said, "The defendant could have had the gun someplace else, in her suitcase or concealed somewhere on her person and put it in her purse at a later date."

"Mr. Mason took her suitcase," Stella Grimes said, "to smuggle it out of the hotel. She was to take with her nothing but her purse and a black sort of overnight bag."

"And that gun could have been in the overnight bag?"

"It could not."

"Why not?"

"Because that bag was full of money with which to pay a blackmailer."

"How much money?"

"I didn't count it," she said, "but it was full of money. I saw that much."

Floyd hesitated a moment, then said, "I guess that's all."

"If the Court please," Mason said, "I notice that an officer has handed the bailiff an overcoat. I believe this is the overcoat that was taken from Mr. Cassel's closet, the one which didn't fit him?"

"*I* don't know that it didn't fit him," Floyd snapped.

"We'll very soon find that out," Mason said. "Mr. Ballard, will you come forward and be sworn, please."

Ballard, a very short, thick-set individual in his early forties, came to the witness stand, moving with surprising swiftness and agility for one of his build.

He gave his name, address, occupation, age, and then turned to face Mr. Mason.

"You knew Moray Cassel in his lifetime?"

"Yes, sir."

"How long had you known him?"

"About seven years."

"What is your occupation?"

"I am a custom tailor."

"Did you make clothes for Mr. Cassel?"

"I did."

"How many clothes did you make?"

"Heavens, I don't know. He seldom kept a suit over six months, and I know that he had a very extensive wardrobe. I made literally dozens of suits for him."

"And you kept his measurements on file?"

"Certainly. I didn't want to have to measure him

every time he came in. He would pick out the material,
tell me what he wanted, and I would have the clothes
ready for the first fitting within a few days."

"I show you an overcoat which I will mark for purposes of identification as Defendant's Exhibit Number
One and ask you if you made that overcoat."

The witness fingered the overcoat. "I certainly did
not."

"I ask you if that overcoat could have been worn by
Moray Cassel."

The witness pulled a tape measure from his pocket,
made a few swift measurements, then shook his head.
"Moray Cassel would have been lost in that overcoat,"
he said.

"Cross-examine," Mason said.

"I certainly have no questions about this overcoat of
this witness," Floyd said.

Mason said, "In view of the fact that this overcoat
which has been marked for identification as Defendant's Exhibit Number One is one that was produced by
the prosecution as having been found in the closet in
Moray Cassel's apartment, I now ask that this be introduced in evidence as Defendant's Exhibit Number One."

"Objected to as wholly incompetent, irrelevant, and
immaterial," Floyd said.

"I would be inclined to think so," Judge Elliott said,
"unless counsel believes it can be connected up. The
Court would be glad to hear your theory of the case,
Mr. Mason."

Mason said, "Before I give my theory of the case, I
would like to have this overcoat tried on by someone

who will fill it out. I have two witnesses here in court whom I expect to use. I think they will be willing to volunteer. Mr. Franklin Gage, will you step forward, please, and try on this overcoat?"

Franklin Gage hesitated, then got to his feet, came forward, took the overcoat, looked at it, and put it on. It instantly became apparent that the sleeves were too short and the overcoat too full.

"That won't do," Mason said. "Mr. Homer Gage, will you step forward please and put on the coat?"

"I see no reason to do so," Homer Gage said.

Mason looked at him in some surprise. "Is there any reason why you *don't* want to?"

Homer Gage hesitated for a moment, then said, "All right. It looks like it's about my size, but I've never seen it before."

He stepped forward and put on the overcoat. It instantly became apparent that the coat was a perfect fit.

"Now, then, Your Honor," Mason said, "I will give the Court my theory about the overcoat. . . . Thank you very much, Mr. Gage. You may take the coat off."

Homer Gage squirmed out of the overcoat as though he had been scalded.

Mason folded the overcoat and put it over his right arm.

"Now then, Your Honor," he said, "if a person approaches a man who is armed and dangerous and wants to be absolutely certain that he gets the drop on him, he must necessarily have a gun in his hand, cocked and ready to fire.

"The best way to do this without being detected is

to have a folded overcoat over the right hand, which can hold the gun under the folds of the overcoat. . . . If you'll hand me the gun which is the exhibit in the case, Mr. Bailiff . . . thank you. I will illustrate to the Court how it can be done."

Mason folded the coat, placed it over his right arm, and held his hand with the gun in it just under the folded overcoat.

"Now then, if the Court please, I will make my opening statement. It is my belief that a young woman who was a friend of a girl who worked with Moray Cassel got into that condition which is generally known as being 'in trouble.' I believe that an executive for the Escobar Import and Export Company was responsible for that condition. I will refer to this man as Mr. X.

"Moray Cassel was a very shrewd, adroit blackmailer. He found out about what was happening and what company the man worked in. He wasn't too certain of some of the facts, but he saw an opportunity to make a few easy dollars. I believe the young woman had no part in the blackmail scheme.

"She had gone to some other state to have her baby. But one of Cassel's scouts learned of the facts in the case and probably knew that the young woman used a code in communicating with her lover. Mail was probably addressed simply to thirty-six-twenty-four-thirty-six, Escobar Import and Export Company, and signed the same way—and these may well have been the measurements of the young woman in the case.

"So Moray Cassel took a chance on making some quick and easy money. He wrote a letter to the Escobar

Import and Export Company and probably said something to the effect that if thirty-six-twenty-four-thirty-six wanted to escape a paternity suit it was incumbent to have five thousand dollars in spot cash. He probably said he was related to the young woman.

"Mr. X was married. He couldn't afford to have the true situation come out. His marriage was not a happy one and he knew that his wife would sue for divorce and for large alimony if she could find some good legitimate reason to prove infidelity.

"So Mr. X went to Edgar Douglas and persuaded him for a financial consideration to pretend to be the man responsible for the woman's condition, to go to Los Angeles and make the payment to Moray Cassel. He furnished Edgar Douglas with five thousand dollars in cash with which to make that payment.

"It happened, however, that when Edgar Douglas was getting his car filled with gas, preparatory to his trip to Los Angeles, he became involved in an automobile accident which rendered him unconscious and he remained unconscious until the time of his death.

"Mr. X, knowing that Moray Cassel was getting impatient, didn't dare to try to find another stooge. He took five thousand dollars in cash, but he also took a gun, which as it happened, although he probably didn't know it at the time, was a gun belonging to Edgar Douglas. He went to Los Angeles feeling that he would make a pay-off if he could be absolutely certain that there would only be one pay-off. If he couldn't be certain there would only be one pay-off, he intended to kill the blackmailer.

"He went to Moray Cassel's apartment. They had a conversation. Mr. X was a man of the world. He knew a blackmailer when he saw him, and Moray Cassel was a shrewd blackmailer who knew a victim who would be good for any number of payments when he encountered him.

"Very calmly, very deliberately, Mr. X killed Moray Cassel, left the gun on the floor in a pool of blood, and returned to San Francisco.

"The defendant entered the apartment some time later, found a gun which she recognized as her brother's gun on the floor in a pool of blood. She hastily washed off the blood, wiped the gun with a damp rag, put it in her purse, and returned to San Francisco."

Judge Elliott leaned forward. "How did this Mr. X get hold of the gun that belonged to Edgar Douglas?" he asked.

Mason looked at Joyce Baffin and said rather kindly, "Edgar Douglas was a nut on guns and on the protection of his women. He wanted any woman in whom he was interested to know how to shoot and loaned one young woman his gun for target practice. I think that Mr. X probably had some influence over the woman to whom Edgar Douglas had last loaned his gun. He may have seen it in her apartment. . . . Do you care to make any statement, Miss Baffin?"

Homer Gage got up and said, "I guess everybody's done with me," and started hurrying out of the courtroom.

Judge Elliott took one look at the white-faced Joyce Baffin, at Homer Gage, and said to the bailiff, "Stop that man! Don't let him out of the door. This Court is going to take a half-hour recess and the Court suggests that the Deputy District Attorney in charge of this case use that half hour to advantage—bearing in mind, of course, that the parties are to be advised of their constitutional rights in accordance with the recent decisions of the United States Supreme Court.

"Court will recess for thirty minutes."

Chapter Eighteen

MASON, Della Street, Paul Drake, Franklin Gage, and a starry-eyed Diana Douglas were gathered in the private dining room at Giovani's.

"How in the world did you ever get all that figured out?" Diana asked.

Mason said, "I had to put two and two together and then find another two that seemed to fit into the picture. A net shortage of ten thousand dollars in the revolving cash fund indicated that there could well have been *two* withdrawals of five thousand dollars each. With Edgar dead there was no need to explain the first five-thousand-dollar shortage. The explanation would be that Edgar was an embezzler and he might as well have been pegged for a ten-grand theft as for five thousand. . . . Actually, I don't think your nephew would ever have given himself away, Mr. Gage, if it hadn't been for your presence."

"It is a tremendous shock to me," Franklin Gage said. "I had no idea . . . no idea at all of what was going on."

"Of course," Mason said, "handling it as we did, Ralph Gurlock Floyd wanted to button the whole thing up quick. He didn't want to be characterized in the press as one who had prosecuted an innocent person. Therefore, he was willing to make a deal with your nephew for a plea of guilty to second-degree murder and call everything square."

Diana said, "I know that my brother wouldn't have had anything to do with getting this young woman— I mean, because of . . . well, the way you said."

Mason said, "But I couldn't count on that. I was working fast and I didn't dare to share your faith without the evidence of that overcoat.

"Apparently, Homer Gage was in a situation which could have cost him his position, his social prestige, and a lot of alimony. Moray Cassel found out about it and put the bite on him, but Moray Cassel wasn't entirely certain of his man. He knew that he was an executive in the Escobar Import and Export Company, that the woman in the case prided herself on her perfect measurements and that the man used to address her as 'Dear Thirty-six-twenty-four-thirty-six.' So Cassel used those code words in putting the bite on his victim.

"And," Mason went on with a smile, "Diana tried to live up to the description."

Diana blushed. "I did the best I could without seeming to overdo it."

"So," Mason went on, "Homer Gage made a deal with Edgar by which Edgar was to take the rap, so to speak. He was to go down and identify himself as the culprit, state that he had no funds anywhere near the amount in question but that he had embezzled some funds from the company and was going to try to make restitution before the shortage was noticed.

"In that way, Moray Cassel would have very probably been content with the one payment. . . . Of course, if Cassel suspected that his real target was a prosperous executive of the company, he would have kept on making demands. And that is why Moray Cassel is dead.

"When Edgar had his accident and nothing was said about the five thousand dollars Homer Gage had given him, there was nothing for Homer Gage to do except take another five thousand out of the rotating cash fund and make a trip to Los Angeles to size up the man with whom he was dealing. He very definitely intended to make a payment if he felt he could make one payment and get out. And he very definitely intended to commit murder if he couldn't make a deal.

"He had that overcoat with him and he became afraid he'd be noticed if he wore or carried an overcoat on a very warm, sunny day so he cut the labels out of the overcoat, and when he had finished with the killing, he simply hung the overcoat in with Moray Cassel's clothes and tossed Edgar's gun down on the floor."

"But what," Franklin Gage asked, "became of the five thousand dollars which was given to Edgar by my nephew?"

Mason said, "Diana recovered that, thought that the blackmail involved her brother's reputation, came to Los Angeles to pay off, and then, following my advice, deposited the money in cash in San Francisco, getting a cashier's check payable to Diana Douglas as trustee."

Franklin Gage thought for a minute, then said, "I think, under the circumstances, the best thing you can do with that check, Diana, is to endorse it over to Mr. Mason for his fees in the case."

There was a moment's silence, then Paul Drake pressed the button. "Hold still, everybody, we're going to have a drink to that," he said.

Diana Douglas smiled at Perry Mason. "You have the check," she said.

And Franklin Gage, producing a fountain pen from his pocket, said, "And I have the pen."